"You've got grit, Rayna," he said.

"I'll give you that. I don't know anybody brave or foolish enough to attempt what you're suggesting."

"You're saying you won't show me a route?"

"A route is the least of your problems. Haven't you heard? The governor's declared a state of emergency."

"I'm doing this with or without your help."

He didn't doubt her for one second. "Fine. I have some forest service maps in the truck."

She sighed, and the starch went out of her. "Thank you."

A bell rang from the direction of the house, the same bell the Deweys had used for generations to call the family inside for a meal.

"Grandma has breakfast ready." Rayna pushed off the stall door and started forward. "Let's go. You can finish cleaning the stalls later."

Aden went with her, his appetite having deserted him. He couldn't decide if finding her a route to drive the cattle was helping her or sending her straight into danger.

Wildfire Threat

CATHY McDAVID

LOVE INSPIRED
INSPIRATIONAL ROMANCE

LOVE INSPIRED®
INSPIRATIONAL ROMANCE

ISBN-13: 978-1-335-42705-2

Wildfire Threat

Recycling programs
for this product may
not exist in your area.

Love Inspired
22 Adelaide St. West, 41st Floor
Toronto, Ontario M5H 4E3, Canada
www.LoveInspired.com

Printed in U.S.A.

For by grace are ye saved through faith;
and that not of yourselves: it is the gift of God.
—*Ephesians* 2:8

To my wonderful son Clay.
You helped bring this book to life with your
knowledge of the outdoors, ranching and cattle.
Thanks for letting me bounce ideas off you and
setting me straight when they just wouldn't work.
I love you to pieces.

Chapter One

Aden Whitley stepped out of his truck and into a cloud of smoke thick and heavy enough to fell a man twice his size. Heated particles seared his damaged lungs, stung his eyes and blurred his vision. A vile taste coated his throat, impossible to swallow down despite repeated attempts. Leaning against the driver's side door, he removed a bandanna from his pocket and tied it around his nose and mouth. The protection provided only min imal relief.

He couldn't stay out in these conditions much lon ger. Not after the severe smoke inhalation he'd suffered this morning and not without adequate personal protective equipment.

From his elevated vantage point, he had a clear view across the valley to Saurus Mountain, so named for the dinosaur fossils discovered there by prospectors in the early 1900s. Towering flames spiked and dipped along the mountaintop on their path of destruction, consuming every morsel of dried vegetation from majestic pine trees to spindly blades of grass. An enormous cloud of brownish-gray smoke hovered above the flames, constantly rising and plunging like a living creature.

Though fifteen miles away, the fire appeared closer and could be upon the small town of Happenstance, Arizona, in less than a day if weather conditions changed. Law enforcement had issued a level one alert and were recommending citizens prepare for possible evacuation. One shift in the wind and that could become an order.

For now, however, the fire headed in a southerly direction that should bypass the town, though a narrow wedge of flames had broken free and was traveling down the mountain toward the west road. Aden raised his binoculars and studied this new and troubling development. Fire almost always traveled uphill. There were rare exceptions, usually caused by the wind.

If this wedge of fire reached the west road, that could spell real trouble for the town's twenty-six hundred residents. Closing his eyes, he murmured a quiet prayer, asking God to spare the road. Also, to protect the courageous souls fighting the fire. Hotshot teams from all over the state had arrived, and more were coming from Colorado and California.

During his third scan of the area for any signs of unusual activity, the radio sitting on his truck's center console crackled to life. "Ranger Whitley, this is Garver District Ranger Station. Are you there? Please respond. Over."

Recognizing the dispatcher's voice, he reached through the open window and grabbed the handheld transmitter. "I'm here, Pilar. What's up? Over."

He assumed she'd radioed for an update. Aden worked for the forest service as a natural resources specialist, what most people called a forest ranger. He also assisted with search and rescue operations during emergencies. The Elk Creek Fire rated as the biggest emergency to hit Happenstance since a rockslide buried half the town four decades ago.

"It's Rayna Karstetter. Her grandmama called in a panic."

"Is Rayna missing?"

"Not missing. She's up near Three Echo Pass. Been gone six hours. Since eight this morning." Pilar groaned. *"Su pobre abuela."*

"During a fire?" Aden snorted in disbelief, which triggered a racking cough. He buried his face in the crook of his elbow until he could speak again. "What's she doing up there? Over."

"Rescuing some stray cows and calves. According to Señora Dewey, Rayna and the neighbor moved the main herd yesterday from their summer grazing location to the ranch. A few stragglers got left behind. She went back for them this morning. Over."

"By herself?"

"Yes, which is why Señora Dewey is so worried. She says that fool girl doesn't have enough sense to wear a hat in the rain. Over."

Aden agreed. Only a fool would risk life and limb to rescue some cows that would probably find their way down the mountain on their own and well ahead of the fire. But that was Rayna for you. She'd decided the cows were worth the danger. And once she set her mind to something, there was no stopping her.

"How far away are you?" Pilar asked. "Over."

Aden squinted against the smoke and studied the surrounding mountains. He'd grown up in Happenstance and spent the better part of fifty hours a week driving the public, lumber and private roads. There wasn't a trail he hadn't hiked, a cave he hadn't explored or a creek he hadn't fished.

"I can be there in fifteen minutes. Twenty tops. Over."

"Copy that," Pilar said. "I'll call Señora Dewey and advise." She paused. "I know you're not Rayna's favorite person. I'm sure her grandmama appreciates this."

Aden didn't comment. When it came to emergencies and someone's life in possible jeopardy, his or anyone else's personal feelings weren't relevant. "Tell Mrs. Dewey I'll find Rayna and bring her home."

"Will do. *Gracias*, Aden."

He opened his truck door. "FYI, the fire's still moving south along Saurus Mountain." He took another look through the binoculars. "A piece has broken off and is traveling down toward the west road."

"Incident Command Post reported the same right before I got the call from Señora Dewey. Be careful. That's not far from you."

"Any additional containment since this morning? Over."

"None."

He expelled a long breath through the bandanna. The grim news on the fire was expected. Still, he'd hoped for a speedy end. On the other side of the valley, flames mocked him by devouring a majestic pine as if it were kindling.

"Okay, I'm on my way now to find Rayna." He climbed in behind the steering wheel, yanked the door shut and closed the window. Pulling down his bandanna, he said, "Over and out."

"Wait. Before you go, how are you feeling?"

"I'll live."

"Don't joke, *mi amigo*. That was a close call."

Aden had been assisting the wilderness firefighters. While driving a bulldozer to create a firebreak, he'd suffered smoke inhalation and possible chemical poisoning from emissions released during burning. He'd been removed from the job, treated with oxygen and put on limited duty for the next forty-eight hours.

Under normal circumstances, he'd have been sent home to rest. But these weren't normal circumstances. As a result, he was checking on residents and informing them of the evacuation alert, locating any campers or recreationists still in the area and ordering them to leave. He was also helping Search and Rescue—hence the call from Pilar to go after Rayna.

"Promise me you won't overexert yourself," Pilar said. "I know how you are. You hate light duty."

"I'll be careful."

"I'm serious, Aden. You need to heal."

"Copy that." He smiled to himself, imagining the motherly dispatcher's cherub face. "I'll radio in when I find Rayna."

"Good luck. Over and out."

Executing a U-turn, Aden bumped down the washboard dirt road. Plumes of brown dust filled his rearview mirror. Not a single drop of rain had fallen in over four months, making this June one of the driest on record.

Fire thrived on droughts, and nature had provided this one with a banquet. Someone in the media had dubbed it the Elk Ridge Fire after the recreational site where it had started three days ago. A careless individual had completely ignored the no campfire signs posted and lit one, anyway. A small fire, according to him, which—when left unattended for ten minutes—had shot sparks into the nearby dry grass.

Anger ate a hole in Aden's gut. Next to God, there was nothing he loved more than this land. That someone would blatantly disregard rules and jeopardize others was beyond his comprehension. Valuable natural resources would be lost. Property destroyed. People may die. And for what? A campfire?

At the bottom of the mountain road, he came to a stop and let the engine idle. In the sky to his left, a small plane materialized from a cloud of smoke, flying toward Saurus Mountain. A speck at first, it steadily grew. Aden craned his neck for a better view and grabbed his binoculars off the passenger seat. As the plane reached the top of the mountain, it dropped a long stream of bright red fire retardant onto the flames that turned the surrounding air the same vivid shade.

According to the most recent report, the Elk Ridge Fire had burned over thirty thousand acres. That number was expected to double in the next two days, if not triple, before it was contained. And if the wind increased speed or altered direction, there was no telling the extent of the damage.

Aden didn't want to think about that right now. Instead, he'd concentrate on finding Rayna and talking some sense into the woman.

He continued along the road for a mile until he reached the turnoff for Three Echo Pass. He stopped at the base of the mountain and, once more using his binoculars, scanned the immediate area. Roughly a dozen head of cattle grazed in a nearby ravine. Rayna had left them secured between a fence on one side and the ravine's steep wall on the other.

All right, he was impressed. She'd done well and without help. The cows and calves wouldn't remain there long, however. The smell of smoke was making them nervous, and they milled anxiously. Sooner or later, they'd trample the fence in an attempt to escape.

She must have headed back up the mountain for more stragglers. How many were there? Aden swung the steering wheel hard and applied the gas. The engine groaned in protest as the truck climbed the steep road, telling him in no uncertain terms that this was a bad idea.

He patted the dash. "I couldn't agree with you more."

Three Echo Pass traversed a low spot between two mountains. The federal government owned this land and leased it to ranchers in the area with strict restrictions on its use and how many cattle were permitted to graze. Sections were divided by barbed wire fencing, and cattle were regularly moved from one section to another to prevent overgrazing.

The strays Rayna was after were likely on the other side of the fence, making rescuing them challenging in the best of circumstances. With a fire raging in the distance and thick smoke clogging the air, her job was next to impossible.

Nearing the top, Aden slowed his truck to a crawl. He searched in every direction for signs of Rayna and found none. Where was she? He didn't bother radioing Pilar for Rayna's phone number. Reception was notoriously unreliable up here, and people rarely got a signal.

All at once, he spotted a movement through the smoke. Hitting the brakes, he raised the binoculars. Yes.

There in the distance, at approximately eleven o'clock, a large white-and-brown animal stirred. Not a cow—the Deweys raised Black Angus. Not a deer or an elk, either. They would have scattered long ago, having much more sense than Rayna.

Her horse. Nothing else made sense. And if her horse was here, she was, too.

Aden reached for his cowboy hat before hopping out. While not regulation wear, he doubted he'd get written up today for the slight uniform infraction. Dust and dirt coated his standard dark green pants and leather work boots. Sweat stained his gray shirt.

Pulling his bandanna up again to cover his nose and mouth, he trudged toward the pitiful mooing of a distressed cow.

The arduous climb caused a pain deep in his chest and triggered another racking cough, which forced him to stop and rest.

Rayna's horse whinnied as he approached and shifted anxiously in place. He didn't want to be here, either.

"Easy, fellow. Where's your owner?"

Somewhere close by, the cow mooed again, joined by a barking dog. Aden pinpointed the sounds. They came from just over the next hill, behind a cluster of juniper trees fifty yards ahead. He made his way there, his breathing beginning to labor. Beyond the trees, the fence appeared and, beyond that, the form of a woman that could only be Rayna. Any other day, without dense smoke obscuring the sun, he'd have spotted her much sooner.

She stood inside the fenced section, her back to Aden, facing off with a two-, maybe three-month-old calf. Unaccustomed to humans, the calf spooked at the slightest movement on Rayna's part. Nearby, on this side of the fence, his anxious mother snorted and pawed the ground. She wasn't much more used to humans than her offspring. Rayna's blue merle cattle dog paced back and forth behind the calf, periodically darting in and nipping a heel.

"Stand, Zip."

The dog obeyed and backed off…for three seconds. When the cow charged the fence, he began barking again, too excited to contain himself. The irate cow trotted off a short distance, her calf following parallel on his side of the fence.

They could, Aden knew, keep this up all day. Rayna most certainly had her hands full.

He continued his ascent. Rocks and twigs crunched beneath his boots and spindly branches reached out to scratch his face. With each step, his visibility improved, and the scene took on added clarity. If there weren't a fire threatening to destroy the town, if the person was anyone other than Rayna Karstetter, he might have laughed at the antics. But she didn't have a single drop of humor where he was concerned. Not that he blamed her.

Emerging from the trees, he called out, "Got yourself in a jam, I see."

She spun, and in the span of a single heartbeat her expression changed from alarm to recognition to annoyance. "What are you doing here?"

"Bailing you out of trouble."

Aden covered the remaining distance to the fence. Zip bounded over to him. Dropping to his belly, he soldier-crawled under the lowest rung of barbed wire.

Once clear, he squirmed to his feet and danced in circles, yipping at Aden in a bid for attention.

Rayna braced her hands on her hips and glared. "I don't need your help."

Aden bent and scratched the dog's head. He didn't always get on well with people and preferred to keep his distance. Animals were different. Them, he tolerated. Even liked. Zip went mad with joy and fell onto his back, begging for a belly rub. Aden obliged. "He's a terrible guard dog."

"He's also a terrible judge of character. I'm going to have to work on that with him."

Zip abruptly sprang up, a canine jack-in-the-box. He ran to the cow and resumed barking and nipping. She kicked out with a hind leg, but he was too fast for her. Aden imagined the dog, despite his young age and playful tendencies, was an excellent herder. Even so, he and Rayna hadn't been able to reunite the calf with his mother and get them off the mountain.

It happened all the time. Calves were accidentally separated from their mothers. This little guy had likely slipped through a hole in the barbed wire fence and couldn't figure out how to get back. The calf and his mother could have walked on opposite sides of the fence for a few feet, a mile or days. And nothing would make the cow leave her baby, not even to save herself from a roaring forest fire. As Aden watched, she leaned into the fence, mindless of the sharp barbs piercing her hide.

"How long you been at this?" he asked Rayna. "An hour? Two?"

She didn't answer.

"Cows aren't cooperative to start with and this half-wild pair even less so. Admit it, you're outmatched."

She looked exhausted. Rounding up stragglers for hours drained a person. Short honey-brown curls had escaped her ball cap and lay plastered against her damp neck, grime streaked what little of her face he could see above the scarf she wore for protection and her normally ramrod straight posture sagged.

Aden grumbled to himself. Daylight was wasting. He had to get Rayna out of here—along with the cow and calf if that was what it took. He used the only leverage he had.

"Your grandmother sent me."

"She sent you," Rayna repeated, her tone skeptical.

"Technically, she called the station asking for help. She's worried sick about you. Says you've been gone since morning. I happened to be in the area."

Rayna frowned, resisting with every last ounce of determination she possessed.

"I bet a minute ago you were wishing you had an extra pair of hands." Aden extended his. "Well, here they are. We also both know your grandmother has enough on her plate with your grandfather's…condition. You don't need to be adding to her troubles." He gave Rayna another twenty seconds. "I get you're holding a grudge against me. But now's not the time."

"Fine." She spoke through gritted teeth.

Aden fished his leather gloves from his back pocket and slipped them on. He'd won this first round with Rayna. The next one might not be so easy.

Rayna had been wishing for help, it was true. The hundred yards to the gate might as well have been a thousand. But why Aden Whitley of all people? She'd wanted to scream when Zip treated him like a long-lost family member. It wasn't as if the traitorous dog had ever met the man before now.

She supposed beggars couldn't be choosers. Aden was strong and capable, no denying that. And right handy, as Grandpa Will would say. With tremendous effort, she swallowed her anger and resentment and, all right, pride.

"I'm thinking the both of us can herd the cow to the gate," she said. "The calf will follow."

"That plan hasn't worked so far."

"You have a better one, I suppose?"

"Cut the fence."

"Did you bring wire cutters?"

He approached the fence and stopped directly across from her, closer than was necessary. She stiffened at the invasion of her personal space.

"I'm surprised you didn't," he said. "No rancher worth their salt leaves on horseback without a pair in their saddlebags."

Her cheeks heated, much to her consternation. "I thought I had a pair in there. I didn't check before I left. My mistake."

"Fortunately, I have this." He dug in his front pants pocket and withdrew a multitool.

"Kind of flimsy. Can it cut barbed wire?"

"We're about to find out." He opened the tool to a V-shape.

Rayna harrumphed.

Aden bent and took hold of the bottom rung. Avoiding the sharp points, he shoved a smooth expanse into the tool's small jaws. This barbed wire was comprised of two strands twined together, and he worked each one separately, grunting softly as he squeezed. With a ping, the first strand gave, the second one shortly after. That task accomplished, he moved to the next rung.

In the near distance, the cow had swung her head over the fence to nuzzle the calf. The weight on the fence didn't make Aden's job any easier. Zip had planted himself on the ground nearby to watch the goings-on, his long tongue lolling and sides heaving.

With the last strand finally cut, Aden returned the multitool to his pocket. Rayna hated to admit it, but the tool had worked better than she thought it would. Together, they pulled the severed rows of barbed wire aside and created a hole large enough for the calf.

"See if you can maneuver Junior through," Aden said. "I'll keep Mama from interfering."

Rayna whistled to Zip, who burst into action. The calf was reluctant at first, probably recalling their earlier efforts when he'd suffered some scratches. But then something clicked, and he realized the barrier separating him from his mother had been removed. Bawling loudly, he loped through the opening and straight for his mother. The two of them trotted off, eager to be away.

Aden came to stand by Rayna, again invading her personal space, and they watched the calf's attempts to suckle.

Sighing, Rayna muttered, "Thanks," under her breath.

"What did you say?" He tilted his head toward her.

"Thank you." She enunciated this time, uncertain if he hadn't heard or was teasing her.

Turning away, he gathered the top two barbed wire rungs and knotted them as best he could before starting on the next row.

"This won't hold long." He removed his gloves and

returned them to his pocket. "You'll have to come back after the fire and repair the fence proper."

"At the moment, that's the least of my worries."

"I saw the stragglers down below. Are these two the last of them?"

"Far as I can tell."

"You put yourself in danger for a few cows and calves?" Aden sent her a look she couldn't quite interpret with a bandanna covering half his face.

"Yes."

To him, they were a few cows and calves. To her grandparents, they represented a financially secure future.

Rayna and Aden started down the mountain toward her horse, treading carefully on the steep and uneven ground. Aden went first in case Rayna slipped or they encountered a snake. She wanted to tell him she didn't need his protection, that she, too, had spent much of her youth in these mountains. But she was too tired to engage in what would prove a useless argument.

"How's your grandpa?" he asked over his shoulder.

"A little worse every week. His doctor put him on a new medication—it's supposed to slow the progress of the dementia. If you ask me, it's not making any difference."

"I'm sorry to hear that. He's a good man. Decent. Kind. He gave me a chance when no one else did."

Rayna wanted to shout, *And what did you do with that chance? Certainly not stop your brother from assaulting him.* The painful lump lodged in her throat prevented her.

Reaching her horse, she untied the reins from the low-hanging branch and slung them over the saddle horn. Zip had kept the cow and calf moving, though they were eager to put plenty of distance between themselves and the fire and required little encouragement.

"I'll wait for you in my truck," Aden said. "Follow you down."

Her impatience increased. "Zip and I can handle it. We've rounded up fourteen stragglers already by ourselves."

"I promised your grandmother."

"Aden."

Saying his name gave her pause. She hadn't spoken to him in fourteen years, right before she'd left to attend college. She'd talked *about* him on occasion with her grandparents. Rare occasions. She'd seen him here and there during the last six months since returning to Happenstance, always from a distance. But this was their first face-to-face encounter.

"Let's get these two off the mountain, and then I'll help you herd them and the rest to your ranch."

"That's two miles away," she protested.

"The sooner we start, the better."

He didn't wait for her to answer and strode off, his long limbs moving with a natural athletic grace.

Rayna had always found tall men attractive, and Aden was well over six feet. Six-two, maybe? Six-three? She'd definitely had to elevate her chin to meet his gaze, something that didn't occur often with her. In eighth grade, she'd stood above every student at school, including the boys. Eventually, many caught up with and then surpassed her. A small part of her, however, remained that young girl embarrassed by her early growth spurt and above-average height.

Ridiculous, of course, and yet true. More ridiculous that Aden should make her feel at ease with her stature.

A moment later, she heard his truck engine roar to life. Nothing to be done about it, she supposed. He was coming with her. Well, the ride to the bottom would give her time to figure out a way to shake loose of him and continue home alone.

Mounting her horse, she nudged the stocky paint toward where the cow and calf had paused to graze. After every bite, the cow would raise her head and stare at the distant fire. The horse, too. It spoke to his training and loyal nature that he defied his instincts to run and instead obeyed her commands.

"Good boy, Bisbee." She reached down and patted the paint's neck before whistling to Zip. "Away."

The dog raced off, circling the cow and calf and snapping at their hooves. There were those who called Australian cattle dogs by the name heelers, and it fit. Besides cows, Zip herded horses, goats, sheep, cats, small children, cyclists and slow-moving ATVs.

Rayna circled the cow and calf on the other side. She and Zip were an excellent team. She'd purchased him after taking over management of the ranch from her grandparents, and he earned his keep daily.

Aden waited in his truck right where he'd said he would and motioned for them to go ahead. Rayna did, hollering to Zip, "Walk up." He immediately herded the cow and calf down the road.

She tried phoning her grandmother but still couldn't get a signal. Maybe Aden had radioed ahead. She considered asking him only to clamp her mouth shut. Fifteen minutes later, they reached the base of the mountain. The cow and calf hurried ahead to join the others in the ravine. Rayna conducted a count and was relieved to find none had wandered off during her absence.

She was about to dismount and open the gate alongside the cattle guard in the road when Aden beat her to it. Leaving his truck idling, he waited while she, Zip and all sixteen head went through.

"Appreciate the help." She waved to him while he closed and latched the gate.

Hopefully, he'd get the message. And when he waved in return, she thought he had. But nope. He climbed back into his truck and continued behind her at a crawl.

A mile from the ranch, her phone rang, the tone identifying the call as coming from the ranch. "Hello."

On the other end, her grandmother burst into tears.

"I'm fine, Grandma. Don't cry."

"This fire has me in a state."

"I'll be home soon. How's Colton?"

"He and your grandpa are cleaning the pens."

"Good."

Simple, familiar tasks were something Rayna's grandfather could still perform despite the dementia. And at five years old, Rayna's son, Colton, thought the stinky and dirty job was fun. The two kept an eye on each other, which helped.

"I'll have fresh coffee waiting for you," her grandmother said.

"Thanks. I could drink half a pot." Rayna hung up after saying goodbye.

The miniherd traveled at a good clip, encouraged by the truck behind them and the dog and rider flanking them. The instant they spotted the rest of the Dewey cattle, residing temporarily in the pastures behind the ranch, they started running.

Aden suddenly cut out from behind. He drove the quarter mile ahead to the pasture gate, having it already open for the stragglers when they arrived. Once they'd rejoined the main herd, they immediately settled. A minute later, it was as if they'd never been apart.

Rayna trotted Bisbee over to where Aden lingered by his truck. "I'll let Grandma know you got me home safely."

"Give her and your grandpa my regards."

"Sure."

"You ready to evacuate if need be?"

A dry chuckle broke free. "You want to have a conversation with me? Really?"

"I'm doing my job. Checking on residents and passing along information about the level one evacuation alert."

With the cows safely returned, Zip's job was done. He brought Aden a stick and dropped it at his feet, wagging his stubby tail and panting.

Aden picked up the stick and threw it. Zip was off in a flash. He didn't return. Instead, he lay down twenty yards away, braced the stick between his front paws and began gnawing on the end.

"We're aware of the alert and will be ready to evacuate if necessary," Rayna said. "Consider your job done."

"Leave at first word, Rayna. Your son and your grandparents are more important than any property or livestock."

Aden knew she had a son. All right, Happenstance wasn't that large. He'd no doubt seen her and Colton around town like she'd seen him. And hadn't he stayed in touch with Pastor Leonard at church?

"Everything my grandparents have is in those cattle and this ranch. *Everything.*" He didn't need to know her plans when it came to safeguarding them.

"If you need help, call me at the ranger station."

He knew better than to offer his personal phone number.

"Okay." She didn't add, *See you around.* Neither did he. Nor did they wave goodbye.

Aden was just climbing into his truck when the ranch's seen-better-days pickup chugged toward them with Rayna's grandmother at the wheel. Great. What now?

She stopped and rolled down the window, a huge smile on her weathered, yet wise and beautiful, face. "Aden. What a pleasure it is to see you. Come to the house for some coffee and pie."

This could not be happening. "Grandma," Rayna called. "He was just leaving."

"Nonsense. You can spare ten minutes. I won't take no for an answer."

"Grandma. He's—"

"Thank you, Mrs. Dewey. I'd love some coffee and pie."

"Don't you have more residents to check on or something?" Rayna snapped.

"I'm allowed a break."

Rayna fumed quietly the entire ride back to the ranch. She was quite certain Aden had accepted her grandmother's invitation merely to spite her. She dallied in the barn, praying he'd be gone by the time she'd unsaddled and brushed Bisbee.

No such luck. Aden was sitting at the kitchen table when she and Zip entered, sharing coffee with her grandfather and showing his radio to her son while her grandmother beamed at them. Zip made a beeline for the table, where he rested his head on Aden's knee.

Anger surged inside her. What were her grandparents thinking? This was Aden Whitley. Younger brother and likely accomplice of Garret Whitley.

And Zip? He was going to need a new home soon if he kept this up.

"Colton, come here," Rayna ordered, more sharply than she'd intended.

Four pairs of eyes fastened on her. Three held shock and surprise. Only Aden's were unreadable.

Chapter Two

Rayna cornered Grandma Sandy inside the kitchen's spacious pantry. "What is he still doing here?" she demanded in a harsh whisper.

"Looks to me like he's having a second cup of coffee."

"No, in this house. With our family. I don't understand."

Rayna had sent Colton to his room on some fabricated excuse. He'd be returning shortly, however, giving her little time.

Her grandmother set the food container holding the leftover pie on top of the bread box. "We're in the middle of an emergency. Offering Aden a pick-me-up is the compassionate thing to do."

Will and Sandy Dewey were two of the most compassionate people Rayna knew. Rather than argue motives, she changed tactics.

"His brother assaulted Grandpa Will, could have killed him, and he's serving time in federal prison."

Grandma Sandy faced Rayna and propped her ample hip against a shelf loaded with home-canned goods.

"Garret Whitley is serving time for attacking that other prisoner and who knows what else. Not for what he did to your grandfather."

Model inmate did not describe the older Whitley sibling. He'd have been released in five or seven or whatever years on good behavior for the original assault and robbery. Instead, he'd joined a prison gang and committed a half dozen new crimes, adding years on to his sentence.

Rayna poked her head outside the pantry. Aden and her grandfather still sat at the kitchen table, engrossed in a discussion of the fire, the latest weather report and what supplies to take should they need to evacuate. On the one hand, she was pleased to see Grandpa Will having a good day. On the other hand, she wanted Aden gone. The desire intensified a second later when Colton skittered into the kitchen, Zip following and nipping at his ankles.

"Colton," Rayna said, striving to maintain a neutral tone, "I've told you not to run with Zip in the house."

The dog couldn't help his instincts. And while there wasn't a mean bone in his body, he might inadvertently hurt someone.

"Sorry, Mom." Colton's sweet features, so like his late father's, fell.

"It's okay. Go sit with Grandpa." *Not next to Aden.*

Her silent message went unheeded. Colton plopped down in the same chair he'd previously occupied. Aden appeared to have received her message, given his raised brows and nearly imperceptible shrug.

Discussion of the fire resumed. Colton and Grandpa Will were equally riveted with the topic *and* Aden. Zip, too. He sat beside Aden, gazing up at him with doggy adoration.

Rayna groaned with frustration and retreated back inside the pantry. She was met by Grandma Sandy's stern expression.

"Aden hasn't talked to Garret since before his first sentencing hearing."

"You don't know for sure."

"That's what Pastor Leonard told us."

"Hmm." Rayna remained unconvinced. "The sheriff believed Aden was in on the robbery and helped his brother."

"It was never proven."

"It was never *dis*proven. He had no alibi, and old Mrs. Sturlacky saw him that night running home at around the time his brother was beating the stuffing out of Grandpa."

"Your grandpa insisted Aden wasn't there. Joe, too," Grandma Sandy said, naming the local market's owner. "Garret swore he acted alone."

"One—" Rayna ticked off items on her fingers "—just because Grandpa or Joe didn't see Aden is no proof he wasn't there. He could have been outside providing lookout for Garret. Two, Grandpa was severely injured and Joe locked in the storeroom. Their recollections aren't reliable. Three, the Whitleys are tightknit and have lied for each other in the past. That's a fact."

"Aden's had no contact with his family since he found God. They've cut him off completely, which is truly sad."

"You're too trusting, Grandma."

"Aden's a different man. You have trouble accepting that because you weren't here to witness his transformation."

"Leopards don't change their spots."

"Even if he participated in the robbery, your grandfather and I have forgiven him. He's more than made up for any misdeeds he committed as a teenager with all the good he's done. He rescued that couple last winter when their car went off the side of the road and into a snowbank. He also located that lost hiker two years ago."

"He *helped* rescue that couple and was one of two search team members who located the lost hiker."

Rayna had heard of Aden's accomplishments and considered them overrated. Plenty of folks in town shared her opinion. The Whitleys weren't held in high regard. They drank heavily, started trouble, couldn't hold down jobs and were foul tempered. As strongly as Rayna's grandparents believed in Aden's innocence, there were many who didn't.

"You still think of him as that kid who worked here one summer." Rayna crossed her arms.

"I do." Grandma Sandy's expression softened. "Your grandpa and I, we saw the good in him then. Buried deep, but there."

Rayna had seen the good in Aden, too. At least, she thought she had. She'd admitted to no one her secret crush on him in those days—which made what she'd viewed as his betrayal of her kind and generous grandparents all the harder to bear.

"Because of his family's influence, he was traveling down the wrong path," Grandma Sandy continued. "He just needed someone to show him the right one. It's fortunate Pastor Leonard was there."

Rayna didn't want to talk about Aden anymore and snuck another discreet peek at the table. "We should get out there."

"You think you might be too hard on him because of what happened to Steven?"

She closed her eyes at the tidal wave of grief that always accompanied any mention of her late husband. He'd been taken from her three years ago—and *taken* was an accurate description. Steven had died while filling his car with gas not a half mile from their house in Phoenix. A stray bullet from an armed robbery he'd had no idea was in progress had entered the left side of his brain and passed clean through. He'd died instantly, twenty-five feet away from where the wounded store clerk lay.

So yes, Rayna couldn't easily forgive or look past acts of violence. The scars crisscrossing her heart refused to let her.

"You turned from God when he died," her grandma said softly.

"I didn't turn from Him." Rayna sniffed. "We just stopped talking for a while."

"Until you came here."

It was true. The devastating news of her grandfather's dementia diagnosis had shaken Rayna to the core. But then the day came when her grandmother had phoned in tears. Grandpa Will, not remembering that they'd sold off their cattle, had emptied their retirement fund and purchased a new herd without her grandmother's knowledge. Hearing that, Rayna had immediately decided to return to Happenstance.

Her grandparents had needed help running the ranch and managing the replacement cattle until they could be sold in the fall and the retirement fund restored. She was the only family member capable of uprooting and who possessed the necessary ranching skills. Her mom, divorced since Rayna was a child, currently lived three states away and laughingly referred to herself as married to her job. Her mom's sister suffered from rheumatoid arthritis, and her cousins either had other responsibilities or didn't care.

Rayna had refused to let their apathy upset her. Rather, she'd felt God was showing her a new direction and giving her a chance to finally heal. More than that, she could raise her son in the same wonderful small-town environment where she'd spent countless summers, holidays and school breaks while growing up.

"Is that true, Ranger Whitley?" Colton's excited voice carried across the kitchen.

"Scout's honor."

Rayna suffered a small stab of pain when her son mispronounced *true* and *Whitley*. His speech had regressed after his father was killed, and he still sometimes struggled with consonant blends. Twice-weekly sessions with a specialist had delayed his enrollment in preschool by many months and put him behind his peers.

He'd be starting kindergarten in a couple of months at Happenstance's small K–8 school. Rayna hoped he'd fare better there than he had in the Phoenix preschool where he'd been teased by his classmates.

She emerged from the pantry and went to stand by the sink, where she pretended to tidy. Her grandmother refilled her coffee mug and joined the others at the table.

"I was fifteen the summer I worked for your great-grandparents," Aden said to Colton.

"He's an ornery boy, that one." Grandpa Will chuckled and leveled a gnarled finger at Aden. "I can't get him to show up on time to save his life."

Aden smiled for the first time. A tender, sad smile. "I promise to try harder, Mr. Dewey."

"You'd better. Breakfast comes with the job, and we're tired of waiting on you."

Rayna suffered another painful stab. She'd thought Grandpa Will was having a good day. But, clearly, he was in the past and seeing Aden as the troubled teen he'd hired one summer. Pastor Leonard had been the youth minister in those days, as well as a history teacher at the high school. Grandpa and Grandma had done the youth minister a favor by providing a positive influence for Aden.

"How about next time I bring you breakfast?" Aden asked, still smiling.

"Oh, now, Will." Grandma Sandy reached across the table and patted his hand. "Don't you be bothering Aden with that."

"A boy's got to learn." Grandpa Will nodded sternly.

"I wanna learn," Colton piped up. "I wanna run a ranch when I grow up, just like Mommy."

"I'm sure you will." Aden shot Rayna a glance.

She stared, momentarily transfixed. Like her grandfather, she was in the past and seeing a teenage Aden sitting at the table.

A slight scruff covered his cheeks and jaw that hadn't been there at fifteen and gave a rough edge to what was probably a boyishly handsome face when clean-shaven. He had the same brown hair, now cut no-nonsense short, and the same startling blue eyes that could make her feel disconcerted and tingly at the same time.

She hadn't liked it then, and she most certainly didn't like it now.

"You want to learn, too, young man?" Grandpa Will squinted at Colton, his forehead crinkled in confusion.

Oh, no! Rayna had seen this all too often in recent months. Grandpa Will failed to recognize his great-grandson. In his mind, he was in a world where Colton hadn't been born yet.

She sought her grandmother's glance, the worry in it matching hers. Sometimes when this happened, Grandpa Will's anger escalated out of control. He'd yell and slam doors or cabinet drawers and storm off, his way of venting anger at the disease robbing him not just of his ability to remember but large chunks of his life.

"Or I might be a forest ranger," Colton said, his mouth pursed in concentration.

"You could always do both," Aden suggested and ruffled the boy's hair. "You want to see how my radio works?" He picked up the device that had been sitting beside his coffee cup.

"Yes!" Colton leaned forward, his voice filled with awe when he spoke. "Can I hold it?"

"Okay, but be careful."

When Grandpa Will quieted and appeared to withdraw into himself, Grandma Sandy smiled her appreciation at Aden. The potential crisis had been adverted. Temporarily at least.

Normally, Rayna might have bristled at Aden touching and engaging with her vulnerable and impressionable son. But this was by far the lesser of two evils. She'd give Aden exactly five minutes to show Colton the radio and not a second longer—she wouldn't deprive her son of the enjoyment.

After that, she'd shoo Aden out of the house. This ridiculousness had gone on long enough. Her grandparents were softies. She'd be the strong, rational one and see that they weren't taken advantage of again.

Aden knew he should leave. If the invisible daggers Rayna flung at him from across the kitchen weren't enough of a reason, he'd taken too much of the Deweys' valuable time. Besides, he had his own preparations to make. Should the order come to evacuate, he wanted to be free to concentrate on helping the residents of Happenstance, not busy packing essentials.

But he'd needed a break after a grueling day and what could be a long night if he got called in. That, coupled with Rayna's startled reaction to her grandmother's invitation, had prompted him to accept Mrs. Dewey's invitation.

Okay, he admitted, if only to himself. He found her intriguing. And attractive, with that mess of short curls and lovely oval face. But she was beyond his reach, and he'd be a fool to think otherwise.

It wasn't just about him being from the wrong side of town, which in Happenstance amounted to a run-down mobile home park. Or that the Whitleys had always been on a first-name basis with local law enforcement.

He didn't deserve Rayna. Not after what he'd done. After what he *hadn't* done. If she knew, she'd toss his sorry hide from here to the state line, and he wouldn't blame her.

That summer he'd spent at the ranch, he'd liked Rayna and thought she might have liked him, too, despite her being a year ahead of him in school. Then, the following spring, Aden's older brother, Garret, had embarked on his career as a professional criminal by robbing Joe's Quick Stop Market.

Rayna's grandfather had spent a week in the hospital recovering from his injuries, followed by a month recuperating at home. Wrought with guilt, Aden had offered to help out on the ranch for free. The Deweys and Rayna had declined. She hadn't spoken to him again until the day before she left for college and that was to tell him to leave her grandparents alone.

"What's the latest you hear on the weather?" Mrs. Dewey asked him, sipping her coffee.

"The wind's still blowing in a southern direction between twenty and twenty-five miles per hour."

"That's good." She sighed. "The direction, I mean. For the town. Not the mountains. So many acres lost."

He showed Colton the push-to-talk switch on his radio. "I'm concerned about the west road. The fire was making its way down the mountain last I checked. That could mean trouble."

"Oh dear."

The west road was closest to the Deweys' ranch and led to Payson. The east road led to Globe. Both could be treacherous in foul weather, but the east road had far more switchbacks and sharper drop-offs. If the west road was closed, people would be exiting town at the same time and taking the same winding, precarious route. Accidents were inevitable.

"You need to be ready to leave at a moment's notice." Aden shot Rayna a look, silently reminding her of their earlier conversation. "Just because the fire's not in your backyard doesn't mean there's no danger."

"We can leave now that the stragglers have been rounded up, if we have to," Mrs. Dewey said and then turned to Rayna. "You had me scared witless today. Why didn't Billy Roy go with you?"

"He was busy, Grandma," Rayna said, her words clipped.

"Thank goodness Aden showed up when he did. Otherwise, who knows how long you'd've been stuck there?"

Mr. Dewey suddenly roused from whatever fog had claimed him. "We have to get up to the cabin. I'm not going anywhere without my brother's chest."

"Now, Will, hush." Mrs. Dewey patted his hand. "No need to fret about that."

"Woman, how many times have I told you not to hush me?" Agitation sparked from his no longer cloudy eyes. "My brother fought and died for what's in that chest."

Aden had seen the chest, which was actually more of a lockbox. During his summer here, Rayna's grandfather had taken him to the old cabin. The first Deweys had settled in Happenstance during the 1930s. They'd purchased a few acres and a few head of cattle, adding to both every year. Mr. Dewey's uncle supposedly won the cabin from an old prospector in a poker game. No one knew for certain if the story was true or not.

Mr. Dewey's younger brother had retreated to the abandoned cabin after returning from the Vietnam War, becoming a recluse. Most likely, he'd suffered from acute and untreated PTSD. He'd died in 1992 from falling off a cliff behind the cabin. Perhaps he'd jumped. People had their theories.

So, in a way, Mr. Dewey was right. His brother had not only fought for the medals and other war mementos in the chest, he'd died for them, too.

"What if the fire burns the cabin?" Mr. Dewey demanded.

"Then it does, Will," Mrs. Dewey said gently. "Nothing we can do to stop that."

"We can get the chest." He thumped his fist on the table, rattling coffee cups. "What's in there brought my brother home to us in one piece. We need it. To protect us."

Aden noted the anxious looks passing between Rayna and Mrs. Dewey and the discomfort on Colton's face.

"Grandpa." Rayna came over from the sink and placed a hand on the older man's shoulder. "That old suspension bridge across the ravine isn't safe. It hasn't been for a long time."

"We go around, then."

"There's no other way to get to the cabin."

There were ways, Aden supposed, with time and the proper equipment. Two things they didn't have. He agreed with Mrs. Dewey. Saving her late brother-in-law's mementos weren't a priority, no matter how sentimental they were. All they could do was hope and pray the fire missed the cabin.

"Colton," Rayna said with strained casualness. "Why don't you read or color in your room for a while?"

"I wanna stay here."

"Colton," she repeated.

"Please, Mommy."

Aden watched as her internal struggle played out on her face. She didn't want her son to see his great-grandfather's increasing agitation. She'd also prefer to avoid a public parent-child power struggle. Aden considered offering to take Colton outside but kept his mouth shut. His good intentions would be viewed as interference.

He should leave. He had work to do. Campsites to check and residents to visit. Besides, this was a family matter that had nothing to do with him. He started to say goodbye, only to be interrupted by Mr. Dewey.

"What about Harlan?"

"What about him, Grandpa?" Rayna asked.

"We can't leave him behind."

Practically everyone in town knew Harlan, including the six hundred part-time summer residents. A colorful and eccentric character, he'd lived off the grid for as long as Aden could remember in a ramshackle house not far from the Dewey cabin. He and Mr. Dewey were friends, two old men who enjoyed reminiscing together about days gone by. Harlan's stories were always entertaining, if a little far-fetched.

"I'm sure he'll be fine and, if need be, evacuate along with everyone else," Rayna said.

"That's just it." Mr. Dewey pounded the table again. "He won't. Says he's staying put and riding out the fire."

Another round of worried glances passed between Rayna and her grandmother. Colton hunched his shoulders forward and stared at his lap.

Here was something Aden could help with. "Mr. Dewey, how about I contact Search and Rescue and alert them? They can check on Harlan when they're in the area and maybe convince him to evacuate."

Mr. Dewey grumbled something that might have been "Okay."

"There you go." Mrs. Dewey's features relaxed. "Search and Rescue will take care of him."

They wouldn't necessarily "take care of him," but

Aden didn't correct her. What mattered most was to keep Mr. Dewey calm. Especially for Colton's sake.

"Thank you, Aden," she said.

"No problem."

"You're a good man. It's a shame not everyone sees that."

Was it Aden's imagination, or did Mrs. Dewey's glance cut briefly to Rayna?

"You haven't always been treated fairly by folks around here," she continued.

"They have their reasons. I got in a lot of trouble."

"You were young, and you learned your lessons. That's what counts. Your brother's actions, his choices, shouldn't reflect on you." She reached across the table and squeezed her husband's hand. "Is that not true, Will?"

Mr. Dewey frowned and muttered, "I need to feed the animals."

The dementia had once again put him in a fog.

"Well." Mrs. Dewey smiled sadly. "*We* know it's true. Right, Rayna?"

She nodded stiffly, her smile forced. "Thank you again for your help today."

Aden recognized the comment for what it was: a dismissal. He ignored the small slight. He was a Whitley, after all, and had received slights much of his life. It came with the territory.

Granted, he didn't go out of his way to change anyone's mind. Why bother? He often struggled with believing himself deserving of God's grace, much less friendship or a woman's affection. The solitary life of a forest ranger suited him. As did volunteering with Search and Rescue. He could help people, which he believed was his calling, without having to interact closely with them.

"My pleasure." Aden stood. "Thank you for the pie and coffee and the company. Like I told Rayna, if you need anything, you can leave word at the ranger station."

The movement woke Zip, who'd fallen asleep on the floor beneath the table. With a startled yap, he jumped up and shook himself.

Aden patted Colton on the back. "I'm appointing you official deputy forest ranger. Your job is to take care of your mom and your great-grandparents. Can you do that?"

"Cool!" The boy sprang from his chair and pivoted to face Rayna. "Mommy, did you hear that? I'm a deputy forest ranger."

"I did. Wow." She sent Aden the tiniest of grateful smiles.

It lifted him like nothing had in a very, very long time. He nodded in return, not trusting his voice. He'd thought the walls surrounding his heart too impenetrable to be breached and was surprised to find they weren't. A thin crack existed, and Rayna had found it.

"We'll walk you outside," Mrs. Dewey offered and linked arms with her husband to help steady him.

Rayna grabbed Colton's hand. The five of them went out the kitchen door. Zip lived up to his name by immediately racing off to inspect a thicket of nearby bushes.

Aden had parked his green work truck with its distinctive forest service logos behind the house. They strolled leisurely toward it, Mrs. Dewey insisting Aden not to be a stranger and Mr. Dewey still mumbling about feeding the animals.

At the driver's side door, Aden's radio crackled to life.

"Ranger Whitley, this is Garver District Ranger Station. Are you there? Please respond. Over."

He held the transmitter to his mouth. "Copy, Pilar."

"You still in the area of Dewey Ranch? Over."

"Affirmative." He locked gazes with Rayna.

Her grip on Colton's hand tightened.

"You need to stay put," Pilar said. "As of three minutes ago, the fire reached the west road. Repeat, the fire has reached the west road, making it inaccessible. Over."

The news hit Aden like a mule kick to the gut. What he'd most dreaded had come to pass. "Copy that," he said.

"Do not leave the area until further notice. Do not take any unnecessary risks. Over."

"I'll drive the maintenance road. I can be at the station in twenty minutes."

"No. Repeat, we need you there to alert the residents should the evacuation order come. And you haven't been medically cleared to return to duty. That's a direct order from Incident Command Post, Ranger Whitley. Over."

They knew him well. "What is the latest on evacuation?"

"Depends on the wind. We're remaining at level one for now, and I stress 'for now.' One shift in the winds, and that will change. Are you able to drive around and report on conditions? Over."

"Affirmative. I'll leave shortly. Contact me with any updates. Over."

"Roger that. Over and out."

Aden let his hand holding the transmitter drop. No chitchatting on this call. He was one on a lengthy list of individuals Pilar needed to contact.

"The west road is near the cabin," Mr. Dewey said, his eyes remarkably clear and alert. "We need to do something."

"Not that near, Will," Mrs. Dewey assured him.

But she was wrong, Aden thought. The west road was close to the cabin. Close enough, leastwise, to cause concern. Unlike the Dewey ranch, which was south of Happenstance and farther away from danger.

He reached for the door handle.

"Wait!" Mrs. Dewey said. "Where are you going?"

"Figured I'd find a spot to camp for the night."

"You heard that woman. You're to stay put."

"I'll remain in the area, Mrs. Dewey."

"You'll remain right here. Where are you planning to sleep?" She indicated his truck. "In there?"

It wouldn't be the first time. "I have my sleeping bag."

"Camping in the middle of a forest fire? Have you lost your senses?"

"The fire's still a good ways away. I won't camp anywhere near it."

"And what was that about not being medically cleared?" she asked. "Are you hurt?"

"It's nothing."

"You're a terrible liar."

"I suffered some smoke inhalation this morning," he said. "No big deal."

"No big deal, my foot," Mrs. Dewey said. "I'm setting an extra plate for you at dinner."

"Seriously," Aden objected. "I'll be fine."

"Stay." The softly issued request came from Rayna.

He drew back to study her and swore he spotted a glimmer of emotion before it vanished. "Are you sure?"

"Grandma's right. You shouldn't be camping during a wildfire. Especially when you're recovering from smoke inhalation."

Well, apparently she didn't dislike him as much as he thought. "Okay. I accept. Thank you."

Chapter Three

Colton shoved open the pickup's passenger door and jumped to the ground a microsecond after Rayna braked to a stop. Zip followed, leaping from the seat with his trademark excited bark.

"Colton, honey, wait up." She wrenched open her own door. "Don't run."

This mild display of misbehaving was little-boy-payback, she supposed. He'd wanted to go with Grandpa Will and Ranger Whitley to feed the horses, goats and chickens, Colton's favorite chore. Instead, Rayna had insisted he come with her to check on the cattle. He liked that chore, too, but she was a poor substitute for, in his opinion, the most exciting visitor they'd had since moving to the ranch.

He hadn't stopped talking about Aden once, except to complain that Rayna had forced him to come with her. She could relate—she hadn't stopped *thinking* about Aden once.

"Colton, don't grab the fence," she hollered. "You'll cut yourself."

Naturally, he grabbed it with both hands.

She finally caught up with him. By then, he'd let go of the fence to pick up a stick and toss it for Zip. The dog caught the stick in midair and then ran off with it. Seemed both of them were in the mood to test Rayna's patience.

"You'll see Ranger Whitley at dinner," she told Colton, who was kicking the metal fence post and making it twang. "Grandma Sandy's fixing hamburgers. Your favorite."

"And we'll see him tomorrow morning." Colton instantly brightened. "He's sleeping over."

Tomorrow morning! What had gotten into her? Who cared if Aden camped out during a forest fire, even if he had recently suffered smoke inhalation?

Rayna did. She cared. A horrifying image of him trapped in his truck, flames engulfing it and him unable to breathe, had popped into her head. She couldn't let that happen. Even if he had provided lookout during the market robbery, he'd been young and no doubt influenced by his brother.

Her grandmother was possibly—okay, probably—right. Rayna did need to cut Aden some slack. At first, her anger at him had been fueled by seeing her grandfather lying in a hospital bed, hooked up to tubes and wires, his face bloody and bruised beyond recognition. She'd never forget that sight for as long as she lived.

And yes, her grandfather's assault closely resembled the events of Steven's death. Rayna couldn't separate the two and had trouble seeing Aden as the man he was today rather than the errant teen who'd spray-painted her grandparents' church, shoplifted, started fights and been repeatedly caught trespassing in the middle of the night.

"You know what I was thinking about today?" Rayna stroked Colton's hair. The cattle were fine. Coming out here had been an excuse to put some distance between her and Aden and clear her head.

"What?" he asked sulkily.

"I was thinking about your daddy and the time we went to the beach in California. He carried you into the waves, and you laughed and laughed. Do you remember?"

"No."

"Not even a little?"

Colton shook his head and kicked the fence post again. *Twang, twang, twang.*

Disappointment and sorrow sat like a stone in Rayna's stomach. She couldn't be mad at Colton for not remembering; he'd been only two when Steven was killed. What few memories he had of his dad were fading like shadows in encroaching nightfall.

She'd feared they'd disappear entirely one of these days. To prevent that, she kept pictures of the three of them in her room and Colton's room and in photo albums. They regularly watched the videos she'd saved on her laptop, and she talked about Steven whenever an opportunity presented itself.

Seeing her son so drawn to another man—granted, most kids his age were fascinated with people in uniforms—hurt Rayna. She'd wanted his father to always hold a hero's place in his heart. Knowing the unlikelihood of that was like losing Steven all over again.

"Can we go home now, Mommy?"

"Sure."

Rayna gave the cattle one last look and sighed. If the fire didn't force them out, they'd eat down the water-starved grass to nubs in a matter of days. There was only enough hay on the ranch to feed two-hundred-plus hungry mouths for a day. Possibly two. She'd need to move the herd soon.

"Ew, it stinks." Colton wrinkled his nose with disgust on their return walk to the truck.

"Yeah, I know. That's the smoke from the fire."

Rayna shielded her eyes and squinted at Saurus Mountain. Flames covered the top half, their tips reaching high to lick the massive blanket of smoke hovering above. A plane zoomed low to drop another load of flame retardant. Farther off, a pair of helicopters circled, probably carrying TV news camera operators.

Her spirits plummeted at the sight of the wide river of flames traveling downward to the west road. It was just as the woman on Aden's radio had reported. There was now only one, dangerously steep, route from Happenstance. So much for her plans to take the easier route from town. How would she get her grandparents' cattle to safety now? She had at most twelve hours to come up with an alternate route.

Forty-five minutes later, Rayna found herself in the last place she'd ever thought she'd be: at the kitchen table and having supper with Aden Whitley. She closed her eyes and opened them again. Not a dream. He was still sitting there directly across from her. Even if she wanted to hide in the pantry again, she couldn't, not without drawing attention to herself.

Fortunately, Grandpa Will appeared solidly rooted in the present. Feeding the animals with Aden had also energized him. He couldn't stop talking about the fire, the weather, his pal Harlan—Aden had contacted Search and Rescue while Grandpa gathered eggs from the chicken coop—and what would happen, legally, to the campers who'd started the fire.

"That fellow responsible for the Yavapai Fire is serving time and was ordered to pay millions in restitutions," Grandpa Will said.

Rayna was surprised he'd remembered.

Grandma Sandy snorted. "He didn't have two nickels to rub together. Not like the state will ever get paid."

"I want to rub two nickels together," Colton chimed in.

Neither Aden nor Rayna contributed much to the conversation. Twice she'd snuck discreet peeks at him, only to avert her head when he caught her. After that, she focused her attention elsewhere.

Grandma Sandy passed Aden the bowl of potato salad. "Have some more. There's plenty."

He patted his trim stomach. "Not sure where I'll put it."

"Might be one of the last sit-down, home-cooked meals we have for a while if we have to evacuate. Better eat while there's eating to be done."

"Just a spoonful."

Colton snuck Zip a piece of hamburger bun, which the dog gobbled down. Rayna pretended not to notice.

"I'm mighty sorry the west road's closed," Grandpa said to Aden. "But the good thing is you're here with us. We can use the help."

"I agree, Will." Grandma Sandy smiled warmly at Aden. "I think God sent you here for a reason. To aid and protect us. Rayna's capable, but she's one person and can only do so much."

"Yes, ma'am."

"Ma'am?" She laughed loudly. "You're a grown man, Aden. Call us Sandy and Will."

"Thank you."

"Call me Colton!"

Aden bumped fists with him. "I will, pal."

Rayna was torn. If the order came to evacuate, and even if it didn't, they could surely use a strong, able-bodied individual familiar with the area and livestock to move the cattle to safer ground.

The problem was, his being strong and able-bodied also made her leery of Aden. She and her family were vulnerable in more ways than one.

She watched as he entertained Colton and her grand-parents with a story about the time he encountered a black bear while hiking Cutter's Canyon. Aden didn't appear particularly threatening in that moment. If anything, he was…charming.

Her heart skipped half a beat. Nothing much. A brief lag in its normal rhythm. Barely noticeable. She attributed the peculiarity to nerves or indigestion. Stress. She was absolutely not, under any circumstances, attracted to Aden.

"Colton, you feed Zip." Rayna stood when dinner ended and began clearing the table. "Grandma, you sit and relax. I'll do the dishes."

"Let me help." The offer came from Aden.

"That's not necessary. Really."

"I insist."

He would.

"I'll make a bed for you on the couch," Grandma Sandy offered.

Rayna swallowed. He'd be spending the night under the same roof as her and her family.

"I'll sleep in my truck." He carried the empty platter and plates to the counter and set them next to the sink. "I don't want to trouble you."

"No trouble," Grandma Sandy insisted.

"To be honest, I'm not used to sleeping with other people around. Been a long time. Not sure I'm ready to start now."

"But your truck?" She winced. "My back hurts just thinking about it."

"I want to sleep in the truck." Colton had returned from feeding Zip in the pantry.

"You're sleeping in your bed, young man." Rayna used a voice that brooked no argument. "In fact, you're taking a bath when I'm done here." No telling when he might get another one if they had to leave in a jiffy.

"Aw, Mom."

Aden carted the last of the dishes and flatware to the sink. "Once I saw a bald eagle bathing in a stock tank."

Colton's eyes widened. "Wow!"

"There's a cot in the barn," Grandpa Will said. "You can sleep there, if you don't mind the noise and smell of the animals."

"I don't mind in the least." Aden smiled with visible relief.

He wasn't alone. Rayna felt the knot of tension lodged at the base of her neck ease slightly.

Grandma Sandy pushed wearily to her feet. "I have an idea. How 'bout I finish the dishes and get Colton started on his bath while Grandpa watches the news. Rayna, you take Aden to the barn, show him the cot and get him situated."

"Um…" She racked her brain for an excuse and found none. She could hardly refuse and ask her grandmother to take him. Nor her grandfather. His previous energy had waned, and he looked ready to nod off. "Okay." She wrung out the dishcloth she'd been using. "Let's go."

Aden nodded to the family. "See you all in the morning. Good night, Deputy Forest Ranger Colton. You keep an eye on things for me."

Colton threw himself at Aden and hugged his waist. "Good night, Ranger Whitley."

Aden visibly stiffened for a moment before patting the boy's head and then awkwardly extracting himself. Colton scampered off, presumably to his room. Aden moved to the back door, where he waited for Rayna.

She was slow to respond. The sight of her son hugging Aden had sucked every molecule of air from her lungs and left her gutted.

While her heart objected to the idea, in her head she'd always known that eventually Colton might develop a bond with an adult man. Her father, who lived in Tucson and occasionally visited. A teacher. An athletic coach. The youth minister. Steven's brother. She'd assumed, when that day came, the man would be a positive role model for him *and* someone Rayna liked.

But Aden Whitley? Every fiber of her being screamed no, not him! Anyone else. Please.

Rousing herself before her nosy grandmother asked too many questions, she whistled to Zip and met Aden at the door. He waited for her and the dog to precede him outside.

The smell and taste of smoke had increased significantly in the last hour, and they covered their faces with their sleeves on the hundred-yard walk from the house to the barn.

"Are you okay?" Rayna asked when Aden began coughing.

"Give me a second."

Thankfully, his coughing fit quickly subsided.

Inside, dust particles danced in the slanted rays of silver twilight. Bisbee and his two barn mates whinnied from their stalls. Zip sped off after the two barn cats, interrupting their evening rodent patrol and sending them scampering into hiding.

"The cot's in the tool room." She opened a rickety wooden door. "I'm not sure where you want to set it up."

"That corner over there looks good." He motioned to her grandfather's work area.

"It's kind of cluttered."

"I'll move the sawhorses."

She let him carry the cot over to the work area, where he removed it from the bag, relaxing when he didn't start coughing again.

"You need a pillow?" She should have asked that back at the house.

"I have a small blanket for emergencies in the truck—I can use that as a pillow."

Not very comfortable, but she didn't argue with him.

"Okay, then." She turned to go.

"If you really don't want me staying here, I'll leave."

She stopped and pivoted. "Let's be honest with each other, shall we?"

"I'd prefer honesty."

"I don't trust you, Aden. And that makes me wary where my family is concerned."

"Understandable on both counts."

"My grandparents may buy into this new version of

you. I don't. Not yet. I'll need a whole lot more convincing."

"Fair enough."

She swallowed and steeled her defenses against that piercing look of his. "In the meantime, you're stuck here. I expect you to work—no one gets a free ride."

"Of course."

"And lastly. Do not hurt my son or my grandparents. I won't stand for it. And if you do, I swear I'll devote myself to seeing you pay for it."

"I'll consider that a warning."

She ignored the grin playing at the corners of his mouth. "Good. Then we're in agreement."

She marched out of the barn, her squared shoulders hopefully conveying a confidence she didn't quite feel.

Aden stowed the cot when he woke up the next morning, stretching afterward to relieve the kinks. He doubted he'd spend a second night at Dewey Ranch, even with the order to stay put and him being assigned light duty. If the sheriff's office didn't need him, he'd volunteer for another shift with Search and Rescue. Barring that, he'd attempt to circumvent the west road and go home, where he'd finish his packing and then assist with any evacuations in town.

Speaking of which… He glanced down at his grimy uniform. While he carried a change of clothes and a spare toothbrush in his truck, he sorely needed a shower. And a shave, he thought, scratching his bristled jaw.

One lone light shone in the Dewey house. An upstairs bedroom; Aden couldn't tell whose. Ranchers were typically early risers, but it was early even for them. Between his strange surroundings, the uncomfortable cot and his worry about the fire, he'd slept in fits and starts and risen well before dawn. Though, with smoke blanketing the sky, it was hard to tell the precise hour of day. He relied instead on his phone, which read 4:42.

Coffee would be nice, but he'd have to wait until a light appeared in the kitchen window for that. Sitting on a metal stool, he held his radio to his mouth.

"Garver District Ranger Station, this is Ranger Aden Whitley, come in." He waited a moment.

"Copy, Ranger Whitley," a low male voice responded. "This is Garver District Ranger Station. Over."

"What's the latest on the fire? Over."

He and the dispatcher spoke for five minutes, during which Aden learned the sickening number of new acres burned, that the fire remained no more contained than it had been the previous evening and had encroached several miles closer to Happenstance's northern boundary. Winds were expected to increase during the next twelve hours, with a strong possibility of changing direction. A level two evacuation warning was expected at any moment.

"Continue to remain in the area," the dispatcher said. "If you're needed, we'll contact you."

So much for heading home, Aden thought. "I'll drive the roads in sections 127 and 128 later this morning and report back."

"Copy, Ranger Whitley. Stay safe. Over and out."

He next phoned Search and Rescue headquarters and was relieved to learn there were no lost or injured individuals. Maybe he could take lumber road 271 to town. Avoid the west road entirely.

But what if he was needed here? Mrs. Dewey—Sandy, he reminded himself—thought maybe God had sent Aden to them for a reason. Could she be right? She and Mr. Dewey were elderly, and he had dementia. Rayna was only capable of so much. But there were also the countless people in town potentially in dire straits. He had a duty to them, as well.

His gaze drifted again toward the house. Still only one light on. Aden decided to get started on that fair share of work Rayna had mentioned. He had no interest in incurring her wrath.

Thinking of her brought a smile to his face. The smile remained while he fed the horses, goats and chickens. She was a spitfire, for sure. He could have assured her she had nothing to worry about from him. He'd cut off his right arm before hurting her or her family.

He recalled the look in her eyes yesterday when she'd seen him traipsing up the hill toward her. Rayna mad enough to spit nails had been a sight to behold. She probably had no idea how appealing she looked with her cheeks flushed red and sparks dancing in her eyes. And while he didn't like being the cause of her anger, he couldn't remember when he'd enjoyed himself so much.

With the livestock tended, he located a wheelbarrow and scoop shovel and began cleaning the horses' stalls, a job he remembered well from his summer at the ranch.

Bisbee bumped Aden's arm as he dumped another shovel-load into the wheelbarrow.

"You're right, buddy. I have no business thinking about your owner like that." He stopped and scratched the rangy paint between the ears. "She has good reason not to trust me."

He paused, wondering why after all these years he'd been put in Rayna's path. Was it to make amends for past mistakes? Aden tried to believe God had a purpose for everything that happened, even when that purpose wasn't immediately clear. Take his family, for example, or Rayna's husband's death. He closed his eyes and asked God for guidance.

Bisbee snorted and pawed the ground impatiently.

"Yeah, you're right." Aden patted the horse's neck. "Time waits for no man."

The Deweys had two other horses besides Rayna's. A bay mare and a swayback gray, who clearly enjoyed a life of leisure given his rotund belly.

"Move it, will you?" Aden said and tried to muscle past Bisbee with the wheelbarrow. He'd finished cleaning the stall and was ready for the next one. The horse refused to budge, standing squarely between Aden and the door. "I'm losing my patience."

Bisbee suddenly whinnied, the noise deafening at such close range.

"What's gotten into you?"

"I was about to ask you the same question."

Rayna materialized in front of Aden. The horse had blocked his view, preventing him from seeing her approach. His surprise turned quickly to pleasure that he tried to mask.

"Earning my breakfast."

"Hmm." She held a travel mug in each hand. "I brought coffee."

"Thank you."

She set the mugs down on an overturned crate. Opening Bisbee's stall door, she distracted the big gelding so that Aden could exit with the wheelbarrow. He parked it in front of the bay's stall. Removing his work gloves, he bent and reached for a coffee.

"Which one's mine?"

"Either. They're the same."

"French vanilla? Isn't that what you used to drink?"

She snorted. "When I was young."

"Ah." He sipped the rich black coffee. "You've changed. Well, everyone does."

She narrowed her gaze. "Pleading your case already?"

"You're right. It's early. I'll wait until after breakfast."

Having delivered the coffee, she'd leave, he assumed. Instead, she leaned against the bay's stall door. "Any word on the fire?"

He told her what he'd learned from his calls with the ranger station, about the additional acres burned and the winds changing direction, possibly toward town.

"And the evacuation order?"

"For the moment, we remain at level one alert." Aden took another sip of coffee. "But that'll likely be upgraded shortly. The wind's a real concern. It's picking up."

"Which means we should prepare for the worst."

She had that look in her eye again.

"What are you planning, Rayna?"

"I've been thinking about the cattle."

"If you're asking my opinion—"

"I wasn't."

"I'm giving it, anyway." He leaned against the stall door next to her. She shifted but didn't inch away. "Should the fire change direction and head toward town, you need to cut some fences and set every critter on this place loose. Let them fend for themselves. That's the only chance they have of surviving."

"It's not the only chance." She lifted her chin.

He recognized that determined gesture. "You have a better idea?"

"We can't afford to lose any of the cattle, which we will if I cut them loose. We especially can't afford to lose any if the fire reaches the ranch. Scorched and barren land isn't worth much."

"I get what you're saying."

"Do you?" She turned to him. "My grandparents are in their eighties. Grandpa's medical costs are skyrocketing. He may require specialized care at some point. The cattle will give them the resources to pay for at least some of that." Her voice broke with emotion.

Aden resisted the urge to comfort her with a touch or sympathetic word. She'd appreciate neither coming from him. Not to mention, he was kind of rusty in the human contact department.

"There's nothing you can do," he said. "The fire's out of your control."

She swallowed and straightened her spine. "I can save the cattle."

"How?"

"Drive them to Globe."

"What!" Aden stopped himself from laughing. "Are you crazy?"

"Maybe a little. I'm desperate, for sure. And isn't desperation the mother of improvisation?"

"I'm pretty sure you have that saying wrong." He shook his head in disbelief. "It's sixty miles to Globe. You couldn't drive the cattle from the mountain to the ranch by yourself, and that's two miles."

"I've been on cattle drives before. Three times. Grandpa took me."

"Not the same thing."

Starting in the late 1880s, ranchers from the entire valley would round up their cattle and drive them in one giant herd to the sale in Globe. The spectacular event drew crowds all along the route. Eighty years later, cattle drives became obsolete when large transport trucks came into use. To celebrate the popular piece of local history, townsfolk participated in a miniature version of the cattle drive, which drew tourists to Happenstance and boosted the economy.

"There are only about a hundred cattle on those drives and two dozen people."

"Four or five experienced hands will be enough."

"Who? Your grandparents? Zip?"

She didn't answer, and her chin hadn't lowered a single millimeter.

Aden continued trying to talk some sense into her. "If the order comes to evacuate, the east road will be jammed with vehicles. There's no room for two hundred cattle. Be reasonable and cut them loose."

"You're familiar with the roads." She met his gaze. "Show me an alternate route."

"There isn't one. Not for two hundred cattle. A few head, sure. Or four-wheel-drive vehicles."

Again, she didn't answer him.

"Rayna." He knuckled back his cowboy hat and rubbed his forehead. She hadn't always been this stubborn. It had started after Garret assaulted her grandfather. He wondered if it was a self-defense mechanism. Or a shield to hide her fear. Life had delivered her some difficult blows. "Most of those roads are private. And gated."

"I intend to get permission from the owners."

"And if they don't give it?"

"We may only need to get the cattle as far as Tumble Rock. My grandparents have friends there."

"The Overbecks."

"They said we can keep the cattle there for a week. If we can't bring them home by then, I'll either continue on to Globe or sell the cattle if that's our only choice."

"Not for top dollar."

"No. But at least my grandparents won't be left penniless."

Aden was familiar with the Overbecks, who were good people with generous hearts. And, unlike Globe, their six-hundred-acre ranch was less than twenty miles away from Happenstance. A far more doable distance, though still fraught with difficulties.

"You've got grit, Rayna," he said. "I'll give you that. I don't know anybody brave or foolish enough to attempt what you're suggesting."

"You're saying you won't show me a route?"

"A route is the least of your problems. Haven't you heard? The governor's declared a state of emergency."

"I'm doing this with or without your help."

He didn't doubt her for one second. "Fine. I have some forest service maps in the truck."

She sighed, and the starch went out of her. "Thank you."

"I suggest you start making phone calls to those private property owners."

A bell rang from the direction of the house, the same bell the Deweys had used for generations to call the family inside for a meal.

"Grandma has breakfast ready." Rayna pushed off the stall door and started forward. "Let's go. You can finish cleaning the stalls later."

Aden went with her, his appetite having deserted him. He couldn't decide if finding her a route to drive the cattle was helping her or sending her straight into danger.

Chapter Four

Rayna crammed another can of peaches into the plastic storage bin, moving aside the beans to make room. According to the latest news, experts were predicting yet another change in the wind's direction. The fire could potentially put the ranches and vacation homes northwest of Happenstance at grave risk. As of an hour ago, local law enforcement had officially issued the level two evacuation warning—high probability of a need to evacuate.

Like most of the town's residents, they were abiding by the warning and readying to leave. A few remained optimistic and clung to the belief the fire would bypass Happenstance. Rayna wasn't taking the risk even though her grandparents' ranch was situated in the southern valley and not in the fire's projected path. Frankly, she'd leave now if she had even one person to help drive the cattle. So far, she'd struck out.

It was a tense, worrisome waiting game that had everyone on edge and weighing their options. She'd just ended a call with their neighbor, Billy Roy. He and his family were evacuating shortly, immediately after securing their home. Rayna hadn't mentioned the cattle, one of her main reasons for calling. Instead, she'd wished him luck and made him promise to stay in touch.

Aden was right. She couldn't drive the cattle alone, even with Zip and with Grandma Sandy driving the truck. Not that she'd admit as much to him.

She'd been somewhat successful in her efforts to contact the private property owners along the route Aden had suggested. Several had granted her permission to cross their land, but none had offered assistance. Why would they when they had their own problems to deal with? She'd considered asking the Overbecks only to change her mind. They would already be going above and beyond by letting Rayna's family keep the cattle on their ranch for a week.

She loaded a large pouch of homemade beef jerky, a can of tuna and a box of crackers into the bin. Earlier, she and Grandma Sandy had divvied up the chores. Rayna was responsible for the food—her goal to have enough nonperishables on hand for three days—while Grandma Sandy packed their clothes and toiletries.

Shutting the lid on the overfull bin, Rayna slid it across the floor from the pantry to the kitchen, parking it next to the bin she'd previously loaded with plastic utensils and paper products. They wouldn't be eating like kings, but neither would they starve.

She straightened, observing Aden at the kitchen table sitting with his back to her. He'd recently returned from driving the roads and was taking a short rest. It must be helping, for his cough had improved. He'd mentioned returning to duty several times and no doubt would the instant he was medically cleared.

Colton was squeezed in beside him at the table and

Zip snoozed at their feet. She realized Aden had become something of a fixture in the Dewey household these last twenty-plus hours. One of the maps he'd used to determine a route for the cattle drive was spread out before him. He'd also used a program on his laptop to access something called an active fire mapping program.

Only now, instead of searching for routes, he was attempting to teach Colton the meaning of the various lines and symbols. She doubted her son was catching on, but he was having fun. If she let herself, she could almost imagine this was a regular day, one where they didn't live in constant fear of losing all their worldly belongings.

"See that." Aden pointed to a spot on the map. "When the two lines are filled that means the road is paved. When they're not, it's a dirt road."

"What about the Xs?" Colton asked.

"The road is closed. Maybe there's a sinkhole or a fallen tree."

"So we can't take that one."

"Nope. We can't."

Colton swiveled in his chair. "Mommy, come look. This is a dirt road."

Rayna hesitated. Standing close to Aden earlier in the barn had left her feeling discombobulated. The feeling returned when he turned to stare at her.

"Mommy! Hurry."

"Okay. Coming." She reluctantly approached and stood behind the two of them, her hand resting on Colton's shoulder. "Show me."

He tapped the map with his chubby finger. "There."

"Wow."

"You're not looking."

She hadn't been and tore her gaze away from the neat row of damp comb lines in Aden's hair. "A dirt road. How about that?"

After his return a short while ago, Aden had asked permission to wash up outside with the garden hose. Grandma Sandy had refused to hear of it and insisted he use the hall bathroom to shower. At first, Aden declined. Eventually, Grandma had convinced him. As a result, he'd changed into a clean Western shirt, a pair of jeans and cowboy boots. Apparently, he carried an overnight bag in his truck for emergencies. The hazards of his job and volunteering for Search and Rescue, she supposed.

She had to admit, he appeared more approachable when not in uniform. Or was she softening toward him? Hard to dislike someone who was good with kids and fond of dogs. Also hard not to give that person a second chance.

"We can't take this road, either." Colton indicated a different line of Xs.

Rayna was no expert at map reading, but she recognized the stretch of road not far from the family cabin. It was no more than a wide trail and overrun with low-hanging trees.

Before she could respond, shouting erupted from upstairs. Grandpa Will again. He didn't understand why Grandma Sandy was packing their clothes. He also objected to her touching his stuff, to use his words. This recent possessiveness was increasing as his dementia worsened. Rayna thought it was because he had trouble finding an object if Grandma Sandy moved it. He hated losing his faculties and hated people witnessing his struggles even more.

How awful for a man who could once solve and calculate complicated math problems in his head. He must feel like his brain was betraying him.

"Where are we going?" he demanded.

They couldn't hear Grandma Sandy's response, but it must not have satisfied Grandpa Will.

"You're wrong. I don't want that shirt. Leave it there."

This time, Grandma Sandy's response echoed through the house loud and clear. "Will, calm down. No need to get upset."

A door slammed with enough force to rattle the pictures on the kitchen wall. Rayna clenched her teeth, suppressing her reaction for Colton's sake.

"Is Grandpa mad again?" he asked.

She stroked his hair. "We're all stressed because of the fire."

"I guess." Colton kicked his legs back and forth, barely missing Zip's head.

Aden pushed the map toward him. "Think you can fold this for me?"

"Yes!"

The task was beyond Colton's abilities and would keep him busy for several minutes.

Rayna sent Aden a smile, which he returned. And like that, the floor beneath her feet shifted. Thank goodness the table was in easy reach. She braced a hand on the edge as her mind grappled with this strange new reality.

Fifteen miles away, a fire raged that could potentially destroy her grandparents' ranch and their entire hometown. Upstairs, her beloved grandfather fought a battle with dementia he couldn't possibly win. Tomorrow morning she'd be driving two hundred and thirty cattle to Tumble Rock and all the way to Globe if necessary. Lastly, and most incredible of all, she was exchanging warm smiles with Aden Whitley.

She tried to speak and couldn't. As if he knew the effects his lingering gaze had on her, his smile widened.

A second later, pounding footsteps on the stairs roused her. They all three turned toward the door where Grandma Sandy and Grandpa Will appeared, one visibly distraught and the other angry.

"Colton, dear," Grandma Sandy said in a strained voice. "Would you mind going with Grandpa? He wants to fix that leaky spigot behind the barn."

Rayna had seen this before. Grandma Sandy invented small jobs for Grandpa Will that would free her up to finish whatever task he was determined to undermine.

"I don't want to go with Grandpa." Colton pouted. "Can I stay with Ranger Whitley? Please, Mommy?"

Rayna patted his head. "I'm sure Grandpa could use the company."

"I don't need any company," Grandpa Will grumbled and stormed outside.

Grandma Sandy closed her eyes and pressed her palms to her cheeks. "Oh, my."

"Tell you what," Rayna said to Colton. "You can help me with the camping equipment instead."

He pursed his mouth, clearly torn. He liked camping equipment.

Aden picked up the poorly folded map and his laptop. "I should take these to my truck."

"I'll go, too." Colton scrambled from his chair, waking Zip in the process.

Rayna nodded at Aden. He was helping again without appearing to help. He seemed to have a knack for that.

Once they were outside, he said to Rayna, "Have you found anyone to go with you on the cattle drive?"

"I've made a few calls. Pastor Leonard's reaching out to the congregation."

"Rayna. You need to give up this idea. It's crazy and dangerous."

She drew in a long breath. "Not yet."

He stared off at the mountains, shrouded in smoke and their tops ablaze, the longing in his eyes unmistakable. He disliked being stuck here, especially when he could be useful elsewhere.

"You leaving soon?" she asked.

"The west road's still closed."

"And you were ordered to stay in the area, right?"

"I was."

The way he let the sentence hang made Rayna think he considered the order less a command and more of a suggestion. It was the kind of thinking that had gotten him into trouble as a teenager.

Colton suddenly ran over and grabbed Aden's hand. "Please stay, Ranger Whitley."

"I need to work, pal. Somebody's got to report on the fire and make sure all the campers have left."

"Can I go with you?"

Rayna's heart ached seeing Colton with Aden. Her son's response to him was so natural and endearing. Unlike any he'd had with any other man in his life, except for Grandpa Will. And, of course, Steven when he was alive.

"You're supposed to take care of your family, remember?"

Colton kicked at a pebble and sent it sailing.

"Look. I'll stay a little longer on one condition. We give your mom a hand. Deal?"

"Yippee!"

Rayna turned her head to hide her relief.

The three of them went to the tool room in the barn where Rayna and Aden had retrieved the cot the previous afternoon. Most of the camping equipment had been around since she was in grade school, every ding and scratch evoking a memory. They gathered sleeping bags, a tent that may or may not have all the poles, a propane stove and two lanterns, cookware, canvas tarps and anything else deemed useful.

Midway through organizing, Rayna dispatched Colton to check on Grandpa Will. He returned five minutes later, saying Grandpa was fine and the spigot remained broken.

When Rayna and Aden were conducting a final inventory, she sent Colton on a second trip. "Don't forget to ask Grandpa how long he'll be."

Colton dallied, stopping to play with Zip and pet the horses. He didn't want to leave Aden.

"I know I've been a little bristly with you," she said when Colton was out of earshot.

"Bristly?"

"I want to apologize." She squared her shoulders. "And to say I was wrong. I can see you're not the same person you were in high school. Grandma's right."

He contemplated her a moment before answering. "I appreciate that."

"What happened? To change you. Can I ask? You don't have to tell me if you don't want to."

"Not much to tell. I wound up in detention again for cutting class. Pastor Leonard was the teacher in charge that week, back when he was the youth minister. Guess you could say he talked some sense into me about the choices I was making. Took a while. I wasn't exactly receptive."

"He can be very persuasive."

"No kidding. He got me to attend church."

She retied a length of rope. "What did he say to convince you?"

"Actually, he didn't say anything." Aden chuckled. "He beat me at *Super Mario*."

"The video game?"

"The guy has some serious skills. And he turned our games into lessons without me realizing it."

"I'd like to have seen that."

Aden didn't elaborate and, while curious, Rayna resisted pressuring him. For some, their journey to finding God was very personal and private. She instead changed the subject.

"Things were rough for me after Steven was killed. And with Grandpa's dementia... I've had my share of trying days when my faith was tested. Pastor Leonard counseled me when I first returned to Happenstance, and I'm in a better place now than I was then."

Aden paused and gave her that disconcerting look of his. "I'm really sorry for your loss."

The genuine sympathy in his voice touched her.

"It must be difficult," she said. "Having your entire family cut you off because of your beliefs."

"Not the same as a loved one dying."

"You suffered a loss nonetheless." And he'd surely grieved for what might have been and what could never be.

"My family spurned me long before I let God into my life. They barely spoke to me after Garret's arrest and stopped entirely when I moved out."

Why? Because you wouldn't help your brother the night of the robbery? Or did you?

She wanted to ask but was afraid of his answer's effect on her new feelings for him.

"They're the ones missing out, Aden. Don't ever think otherwise."

Their gazes connected and, just like yesterday, her heart skipped a beat. Rayna didn't bother denying the truth this time. A part of her liked him and wanted to know him better.

Her hand inched slowly toward him, bridging the short distance between them.

"My relationship with my family, or lack of any relationship, makes no difference to most people around here," he said. "They think the worst of me and always will. I'm a Whitley."

With a start, Rayna realized he counted her in that group and withdrew her hand a second shy of contact. Fortunately, he appeared too absorbed in thought to notice.

"Being a forest ranger suits me fine. I can do the work I love, protect the environment and help people while keeping my distance. For the most part. You Deweys have been making that difficult."

"Do you mind? Really?"

His earlier smile returned. "No. I don't."

Something like a spark passed between them. Before Rayna could move closer, Aden bent and dropped a small spade into the box. She tossed the rope she held on top of the spade, thinking she must have been mistaken. Colton chose that moment to come skipping down the barn aisle toward them.

"Did Grandpa say when he'd be finished?" she asked when he neared.

"I dunno."

"Well, go back and find out, honey."

"Can't. He left already."

Rayna groaned with frustration. "Did he head inside or is he feeding the animals?"

Colton shook his head. "I told you, he left."

"Left where?"

"He drove off."

"In the truck?" That made no sense.

"Yep."

Rayna's frustration gave way to alarm. "Does Grandma know?"

"I dunno." Colton knelt and began picking through the stack of cookware.

She tried not to panic. There had to be a reasonable explanation. *Please* let there be a reasonable explanation.

"We'd better tell your grandma," Aden said, his voice low and urgent.

She grabbed Colton by the hand and pulled him to his feet. The three of them hurried from the barn to the house.

Grandma Sandy took one look at them and cried, "What's wrong?"

"Grandpa took the truck and drove off."

"Where?"

"We don't know," Rayna said. "The neighbors'? The market? The hardware store?" With sudden insight, she knew. "The cabin! His brother's chest of war mementos. He must have gone after it."

Aden was already in motion. "Let's go."

"This is all my fault." Sandy wrung her hands as Aden propelled them to his truck.

"No, Grandma, it's not," Rayna assured her.

He wished the two women would hurry up. Every second they delayed put Will farther and farther away. Sandy, however, clung to Rayna with desperation.

"If I hadn't sent him outside, he'd be here now."

Rayna patted her grandmother's shoulder. "Don't cry."

"He was driving me crazy." Sandy wiped at her weathered cheeks with a tissue she'd produced from her pants pocket. "I just wanted a few minutes alone to finish the packing. I didn't think he'd take off like that."

"We'll find him." Aden reached for the driver's side door handle. "Come on, Rayna. Time's wasting."

"Okay." She climbed into the passenger seat.

Sandy pulled herself together. "I'll go with you."

Aden quashed that idea. "Someone should stay behind in case Will returns or calls."

"Yes, but…" Emotion overcame her, and she couldn't finish.

"Grandma," Rayna said softy. "Someone needs to watch Colton. He can't come with us. It's too dangerous."

"Agreed," Aden said.

"You're right, of course." Sandy made another swipe at her damp cheeks.

Colton ran up to Aden. "I wanna go, too."

He squeezed the boy's small arm. "It's your job as deputy forest ranger to watch over the ranch and take care of your grandmother."

Colton's posture deflated.

"I have an important job for you. Something only a deputy forest ranger can handle."

"What's that?" he asked dubiously.

"I need you to call your mom every ten minutes and make sure we're not in trouble. Can you do that?"

"I don't have a phone."

"Use your grandmother's. If your mom doesn't answer, wait another twenty minutes and then call the ranger station. Report us missing and tell them our last location. Got it?"

His eyes went wide, and he straightened. "Uh-huh."

"I'm counting on you." Though he spoke to Colton, he met Sandy's gaze across the truck hood.

She mouthed a silent *Yes*, letting him know she understood he was including her in the instructions.

"You ready?" he asked Rayna.

He slid in behind the wheel and motioned Colton away from the truck. Beside him, Rayna buckled her seat belt. He hated taking her along for the same reasons they were leaving Colton behind: it was too dangerous. But she was used to dealing with her grandfather when he became confused and agitated whereas Aden wasn't.

"Godspeed," Sandy hollered after them as they drove off.

At the end of the driveway, Aden stopped to check traffic, noting Rayna's closed eyes and bowed head. He sent a quick prayer of his own heavenward. Please let them find Will soon, safe and sound. According to

Rayna, that old suspension bridge across the ravine in front of the cabin was a death trap. The thought that Will might meet his end near the place where his brother had died decades earlier sent a chill through Aden.

He opened his eyes to find Rayna staring at him intently with an expression he couldn't quite interpret. Not surprise exactly, nor disbelief. More like astonishment.

He'd witnessed similar reactions from people who, like her, only knew the old Aden. The one who'd scoffed at the idea of conversing with God. Unlike those people, he cared about Rayna's opinion of him. An interesting new development he'd explore later when they weren't searching for her grandfather.

"I know we're pressed for time, but I think we should stop at Billy Roy's first," he said. "Just in case Will went there."

"Makes sense." She wound the scarf she'd worn yesterday around her neck and knotted the ends.

Perhaps he'd been wrong about her reaction to him praying. Nothing showed in her face save concern for her grandfather and fear of the advancing fire.

Billy Roy came out onto the front porch of his house to greet them when they pulled up. "Sorry," he said when they'd explained the situation. "I haven't seen or spoken to Will since you brought the cattle down from the mountains."

"Thanks, Billy Roy." Rayna offered him a strained smile. "If he comes by or you hear from him, would you give us a call?"

"Sure thing. But we're leaving in about an hour."

Aden had spotted the loaded truck and car parked near the barn.

"You might see him on the road," Rayna said, even though the likelihood of that was slim.

"If we do, we'll be in touch."

As if responding to a silent signal, the three of them turned to stare at Saurus Mountain. The fire had done its worst, destroying the once magnificent wilderness by consuming every prime morsel before moving south to the mountain's lesser neighbor, Little Saurus. Aden guessed what was going through Rayna's head: fifteen miles from the Deweys' ranch but eight miles from the cabin. Eight miles was a very short distance for a fast-moving fire to travel.

There was often no explanation for the path a fire took or the rate it moved. It could tear through an entire town, leaving some buildings intact while reducing others to crumbling piles of smoldering ash. It could bear down on a house, only to veer in a different direction at the last second. Efforts from firefighters that previously had no measurable effect suddenly produced miraculous levels of containment overnight.

The best experts couldn't predict everything, and Aden didn't try. All he could do was have faith that the evacuation efforts would prove unnecessary, and people would return to find their homes and possessions in the same condition as they left them.

"Stay safe," Rayna said to Billy Roy, and waved as she and Aden drove off.

He could see her mood had plummeted. "It was a long shot," he told her.

"You're right."

At the main road he swung right. There was little traffic for them to contend with. Most travelers were using the east road on the opposite side of town, competing with the many emergency vehicles coming and going with frantic urgency.

Her phone rang, Colton making his first call right on time. Rayna told him about stopping at Billy Roy's and that they were on their way to the cabin.

As they drove, the smell of smoke permeated the truck's interior, aggravating Aden's lungs. He was tempted to lower the air-conditioning, except they'd roast in the sweltering temperature.

"This is my fault," Rayna said as they started the steep climb up the mountain road that would take them to the cabin.

"You sound like your grandmother."

"I should have checked on Grandpa myself. Not sent Colton. He's a child."

"There's no way you or your grandmother could have predicted he'd up and drive off."

"He's done things like this before. Leaving on a whim and telling no one."

"And he was fine, right?"

She groaned, her eyes trained on the road ahead. "That's a matter of opinion."

"What happened?"

"Which time? When he emptied his and Grandma's retirement account and purchased the cattle, two months after they'd just sold off the previous herd? Or when he decided to drive to Queen Creek and help his cousin Ollie with the grape harvest?"

"I didn't know he had a cousin in Queen Creek with a vineyard."

"Exactly. He *used* to go every year to Queen Creek at harvest time. As a *young man*. According to Grandma,

Ollie sold the vineyard and moved to east Texas back in the 1970s."

"Ah."

"Yeah. Ah."

With each mile they climbed, the smoke grew thicker and darker. Ash and floating debris drifted through the air, adhering to the windshield and forcing Aden to turn on the wipers.

Rayna fidgeted nervously, as if sitting still would bring her greatest fears to life. "What if we don't find him?"

"I'll call Search and Rescue and alert them. See if they can spare reinforcements."

"And if they can't?"

"Let's not get ahead of ourselves. There's a good chance he's at the cabin."

She chewed her lower lip. Aden started to reach for her hand only to hesitate. He rarely initiated physical contact, and given her current feelings toward him, she may not be receptive.

Instead, he asked a question. For some, conversation calmed them and kept their minds from concocting terrible scenarios—a trick he'd learned during rescue operations when comforting distraught loved ones.

"How did you find him? Your grandpa. That time he went to Queen Creek."

"The police phoned us."

"He was picked up?"

"Sort of. Grandpa wound up fairly close to where the vineyard had been located. Pretty amazing considering he hadn't been to Queen Creek in…fifty-odd years. On top of that, it was a three-hour drive, the majority of that freeway. The original land was long ago turned into a housing subdivision. The developers built a mile-long green belt and a park for the residents. He got as far as the park before becoming completely disoriented. Rather than continue, he pulled into a shady spot beneath a tree and just sat there in the truck. Some of the moms at the park with their kids became suspicious and convinced a maintenance man to go over and talk to Grandpa. The man thought he was drunk or crazy and called 9-1-1. The police arrived and, fortunately, one of the officers suspected Grandpa had dementia or maybe a medical condition. Grandpa surrendered his wallet, and the officer found a phone number to the ranch, which he called."

"That turned out well."

"It really did. Grandpa might have gotten into an accident or wandered for days. The police could have charged him with loitering. Instead, they took him to the station, where they gave him a sandwich and a newspaper to read until Grandma and I arrived to pick him up. We've been careful ever since." She cleared her throat and then muffled a sob with the crook of her arm. "Not careful enough," she said when she could talk again.

"We'll find him, Rayna." Aden threw caution to the wind and covered her hand with his.

Not for long. Two seconds at the most. But the connection he felt was both instantaneous and intense. Also, apparently, one-sided. Rayna didn't appear to have noticed. She sat perfectly still, staring out the side window until her phone rang again.

Another call from Colton. The kid took his job seriously. She let him know their progress and location.

Finally, the road leveled out as they neared the top of the incline. Without needing to be told, Aden turned the truck onto the poorly maintained dirt road leading to the cabin. The tires bounced in and out of large pot-holes and over half-sunken rocks. Branches slapped the bumper and scratched the sides of the truck. The heavy smoke and overgrown foliage combined and reduced their visibility to almost zero.

Aden's lack of familiarity with the immediate area didn't help, either. While he'd traveled the nearby hiking trails, he hadn't visited the cabin since he was fifteen. Given the state of the overgrown trees and foliage, Will hadn't been here, either. Aden wondered how much, or how little, money the Deweys could get for selling the cabin, assuming it survived the fire. According to Rayna, her grandparents could sorely use the money.

They breached a wall of interlocking branches, the limbs scraping along the roof of the truck. Directly ahead of them lay the suspension bridge with its loose and rotted boards—half of them missing—and frayed ropes.

And not a single sign of Will or his truck.

"Oh, God! He's not here," Rayna cried and leaned forward, straining against the seat belt harness. "Maybe we should get out and look."

"Hold on," Aden bit out more sharply than he'd intended.

Grabbing his binoculars, he adjusted the focus. Only one road led to the cabin, and they'd driven it. If Will's truck wasn't here, then neither was he. But Aden double-checked just to be sure.

"Do you see him?" Rayna asked, her panic visibly rising.

"No."

"Where can he be?"

Aden grabbed his phone from the holder in the console and pressed the speed dial for Search and Rescue. The call failed to connect. No bars!

He tossed down the phone. "I'll radio Garver District Ranger Station. Any idea where he might have gone? They'll want some leads."

The moment Aden asked the question he knew the answer. Rayna, too, given the light of awareness in her expression.

They both spoke at the same time. "Harlan's!"

A minute later, they were tearing down the mountain at a speed just this side of unsafe. Midway to the bottom, they reached a junction with another road turning north, toward the fire. They continued west.

"I was so sure Grandpa went to the cabin." Rayna forced the words through clenched teeth.

"Me, too," Aden swerved to miss a boulder. "Does Harlan have a cell phone?"

"Are you joking? He doesn't even have an oven. Unless you count that solar box contraption he uses to bake biscuits."

"Guess we don't call him, then."

"Guess not."

The truck hit a particularly deep pothole and bounced a good foot off the ground. Rayna didn't say a thing and held tightly on to the grab handle beside her head when they dropped like a ton of bricks. Aden righted the front wheels when the truck nearly went off the road.

"Sorry about that," he said.

"Just get us there."

A vehicle appeared from the smoke like an apparition, coming toward them from the opposite direction. Aden slowed and opened his window. Sticking his arm out, he flagged the driver, who slowed to a stop alongside them.

"Have you spotted an old white Ford pickup in the last hour heading west?" he asked the driver.

"I did," the woman answered. "'Bout thirty minutes ago, I'd say."

"You by chance recognize the driver?" Rayna hollered through the window. "Will Dewey?"

"No." The woman shook her head. "Visibility is awful, and he was driving really fast."

"Are you planning to evacuate?" Aden asked.

"In the morning. Just made a last run to the market for supplies."

"Okay. Thanks for the help." He waved and eased ahead. "Take care out there."

"You, too."

He and Rayna continued on the road, once again going slightly faster than was prudent. Halfway to Harlan's, Aden's radio went off.

"Garver District Ranger Station. Come in, Ranger Whitley."

Recognizing Pilar's voice, he held the transmitter to his mouth and pressed the button. "Ranger Whitley here. Over."

"Incident Command Post just confirmed," she said in a this-is-business voice. "Fire at the west road has been contained. It is now open for access. Repeat, the west road is open for access."

"Copy that."

"They also report the winds are on a course due southwest. Over."

Southwest. Aden didn't have to take his eyes off the road to know Rayna's reaction. She was terrified.

"What can I do? Over."

"See that the ranchers and residents in your area are alerted. Inform the sheriff's department of anyone who isn't planning on evacuating should we go to a level three."

"Affirmative. I'll get on that as soon as we find Will Dewey. Over."

"He's missing? *Ay no.*"

"We suspect he's at Harlan's." Aden sent Rayna a glance. "I'll be in touch if we don't locate him. Over and out."

The twisting and bumpy drive leading to the recluse's home wasn't much better than the one to the cabin. Aden didn't let up on the gas once. Cresting the last hill, they immediately spotted the Dewey pickup parked in front of Harlan's miserable excuse for a house.

Will must have heard them for he emerged from behind the house, a garden hose in his hands and water spraying from the nozzle. He took one look at them, frowned and executed an immediate about-face.

Rayna slumped in her seat and released a huge, shaky sigh. "Thank you, Lord."

At that moment, her cell phone rang. With trembling fingers, she answered Colton's call. "Hi, sweetie. We found Grandpa. He's at Harlan's…Yes, tell Grandma. Is she there?…Put her on…I will, but first let me talk to Grandma."

While she updated Sandy, Aden stepped out of the truck and visually assessed the situation.

"I'm not sure, Grandma," he heard Rayna say from her side of the truck. "We just got here. I haven't talked to him yet, but he looks fine…Right. I will. We'll hog-tie him if we have to and be home in a jiffy…Yep, I'll let Aden know." She gave her grandmother an update on the fire before disconnecting.

Aden watched Harlan drive an older model ATV with a grader attached to the back in wide circles around the house, mowing down every bit of vegetation and leaving only bare ground in its wake. Will reappeared from around the corner of the house, his arm moving in an up-and-down arc as he soaked the exterior with water. Even from this distance, Aden recognized the steely determination in the other man's eyes.

Hog-tie him? Home in a jiffy? Naw. Aden doubted Will would go anywhere until the firebreak was complete and Harlan's house secured against the fire. Given the two old men's slow progress, that might be a while.

Chapter Five

"Grandpa, we have to go," Rayna pleaded. "Grandma and Colton are waiting for us."

"No can do, kiddo." He ignored her and continued spraying water onto the side of Harlan's house.

"The authorities have issued a level two evacuation warning."

"All the more reason to stay."

"What about us? We have to finish packing."

Rayna had expected to find her grandfather confused and disoriented and mentally living in a random day from the past. She'd assumed she would lead him like a child to the truck and drive him home. Instead, she was confronting a completely clearheaded and very determined man who insisted he was going to help his buddy prepare to, as Harlan had said, "Ride out the fire."

Who did that? The mere thought of it sent a wave of terror crashing over Rayna as she pictured flames consuming the dilapidated structure and everything inside it as if it were made of paper and straw.

"Harlan can evacuate with us."

"He won't."

They were going in circles, having had this same argument twice already in the last ten minutes. All the while the fire was moving closer and closer, though possibly not as quickly in real life as in Rayna's imagination. Acute anxiety did that to a person, she supposed, distorted time and distance.

She glanced over at Aden. He and Harlan were standing by the ATV, gesturing and talking about...she had no clue. Grandpa Will resumed soaking the house with the garden hose. A well fifty yards away atop a small hill supplied water via an underground line. Gravity did the work, pushing water through the line to a spigot protruding from the ground and out the hose in a weak spray. Soaking the entire house would take an hour, if not longer.

Harlan's electricity was supplied by two large solar panels mounted on frames beside the house or, in cases of emergency, a gasoline-powered generator. Most of what he needed to survive came from the land. He grew his own vegetables, which he canned and stored, in a kitchen garden. A half dozen chickens occupied a coop beside the shed. During summers, he collected wild berries in the surrounding woods. And he harvested apples in the fall from a pair of ancient trees behind his property. The nearby stream dumped into a nice fishing hole about a mile down the mountain. Harlan made the trek there once or twice a week. He gathered logs and kindling for heating and cooking, bringing them home on the ATV.

Whenever he needed money above and beyond his monthly social security payment, he worked odd jobs or sold handmade footstools to a tourist shop in town. His only sources of entertainment were books, magazines and an old radio—he loved listening to sports. At Christmastime, people from town left packages containing food, clothing, blankets and other necessities for him at the end of his driveway.

One way or another, he managed. But even a resourceful individual like him couldn't battle a wildfire on his own.

Rayna tried again to reason with her grandfather. "Grandma's worried sick about you."

"I said, I'm not leaving Harlan to finish alone. I'll go when the work's done."

"Grandpa—"

"If you keep pushing me, young lady, I just might stay here and take my chances with the fire."

She couldn't help herself and started to cry. This wasn't what she'd planned. They'd found Grandpa. He was supposed to come home with them. Then, tomorrow, they'd leave to drive the cattle to Tumble Rock.

"Hey, Rayna."

Wiping at her damp eyes, she composed her features and turned to face Aden. "Yeah?"

"You have a second?"

"Sure." She put a hand on her grandfather's arm. "Stay here, Grandpa. Don't go anywhere. I'll only be a minute."

He grumbled under his breath and moved to the next section of the house, waving the hose in a wide arc.

"What's up?" she asked Aden, her tone brusque. At his raised brows, she explained, "It's not you. Grandpa's trying my patience."

"From what Harlan tells me, I doubt we'll convince your grandfather to leave without first making sure everything's been done to secure the house and property."

She didn't like the sound of that. "Define *everything*."

"The firebreak completed. The house and shed watered down. The roof cleared of dried leaves and debris. Any holes sealed, if that's even possible. I have to see what kind of building materials Harlan has around here."

"We're not a crew. We're four people, two of whom are old men. Plus, we don't have time for this. You know that better than anyone."

"You want your grandfather to leave with us or not?"

Rayna pressed her fingers to her temples, allowing her emotions to get the best of her for just a moment.

"The longer we stand here talking," Aden said gently, "the longer it will take us to finish."

She pulled herself together and sighed. "What do you want me to do?"

"Harlan will finish the firebreak with the ATV. I'll clear and patch the roof as best I can. Your grandpa can continue with the watering. You remove any items that'll burn from around the house. Those wooden chairs and table on the front porch, for instance. The box of kindling. The planter—"

"I got it."

"Okay."

"Sorry." She grimaced. "I didn't mean to snap at you."

He reacted neither to her outburst nor to her apology. "If in doubt, remove the item."

"How far away?"

"Past the firebreak. Look for anything flammable, outside *and* inside the house. The shed, too. Propane tanks, cans of gasoline or kerosene. Lighter fluid and lanterns."

She struggled to keep up with his instructions, her mind in a jumble.

"I'm going to contact the sheriff's department. Advise them that Harlan's refusing to evacuate. Maybe they'll have better luck convincing him than I have."

"Can they force him?"

He shrugged. "It's my understanding the sheriff's department can use reasonable force once an evacuation order has been issued. What defines reasonable force isn't always clear, however. And whether they actually will use it or not depends on how many residents are refusing, their location, if any deputies can be spared and the proximity of the fire."

"In other words, don't count on it."

"The sheriff's department has a lot to worry about right now. They're doing their best."

"I know." She felt the last of her energy drain away. This was all so much.

He took her hand in his, his calloused grasp sure and steady. Similar emotions were reflected in the gaze he leveled at her. Rayna stared—not trapped but rather captivated by him.

"You can do this, Rayna. You're going to be okay. Your family is, too."

When he said it like that, she believed him.

"You just have to be strong for a little while longer."

She nodded.

"I'm not going to leave you. I'll stay as long as you need me." He rubbed his thumb along her knuckles.

There was no compliment he could have given her, no vow he could have made, that would have meant more to her than those spoken words: *I'll stay as long as you need me.*

"I hate having to depend on you," she said, resisting the growing pull of attraction. She may have softened toward him, but this was still Aden Whitley. Someone she didn't know all that well and whom she'd disliked until recently. "I can take care of my family by myself."

He flashed her that trouble-making grin of his before releasing her hand. "We'll argue about that later, when we're evacuating."

The contact hadn't been long, no more than the brief brushing of their hands earlier during the truck ride here. But already she missed the warmth of him and the reassurance his touch offered. How could that be?

"We'd better hurry," he said.

She studied his retreating back. The moment between them might not have happened except for the tingling in her fingertips and the warmth surrounding her heart.

Squaring her shoulders, she started for the house. For the next two hours, Rayna worked harder than when she'd brought the cattle down from the mountain yesterday. Lugging, dragging, shoving, lifting, reaching and carrying. Her back and feet complained, her muscles screamed for relief and her head throbbed. Every ten minutes, Colton phoned. Apparently he'd taken Aden's instructions to heart. Each call, he asked to speak to Aden, and finally Rayna relented during one of Aden's trips down from the roof.

She eavesdropped. Of course she did. Aden patiently answered Colton's many questions.

"Smoke can be different colors. It depends on what's being burned…No, there's not enough water for that.

Most of the animals have already left the area for safer ground…No, they don't stick around…I will when we get back…Okay…Uh-huh. You taking care of Grandma Sandy like I told you?"

He really was good with Colton. Another time, when they weren't rushed and fighting for what could possibly be their very lives, she'd ask him why. Had he worked with children at some point? Was it part of being a forest ranger? Did he want children of his own someday?

Wait! Where had that last question come from? And why would she even consider it? She didn't care if Aden wanted children or not. His future plans for a family were of no consequence to her.

She rubbed her still-tingling fingertips together. All the lifting and carrying must be responsible.

"Here you go."

"What? Oh, thanks." She accepted her phone from him, pretending he wasn't the reason she'd been lost in thought.

They returned to work. A half hour later, Rayna decided there was nothing left to remove and made one final inspection of the house and shed. Aden had finished with the roof, the massive pile of dead leaves and pine needles raked and hauled away. Grandpa Will and Harlan stood at the base of the extension ladder, Grandpa steadying the sides as Aden climbed down.

She should have been paying more attention to where she was walking instead of the way Aden's short brown hair lay plastered to his head when he removed his cowboy hat to wipe the sweat from his face. Failing to notice an old, dried root protruding from the ground, she went down hard when the toe of her boot collided with it.

She let out a loud "Oomph!" as she landed on her

hands and knees. So much for the tingling sensation in her fingertips. Now her entire body throbbed from the shock of impact.

"Rayna, are you all right?" Aden's voice filled her ears.

Wasn't he across the yard? How had he gotten here so quickly? "I think so."

"You hurt?"

She hurt everywhere, but she wasn't sure if that was from the fall or that last heavy wooden box she'd hauled from the shed, filled to bursting with magazines from fifty years ago.

"I'm fine." His strong hand gripped her upper arm and lifted her to her feet. "Mostly embarrassed."

"Rayna." Grandpa Will's face swam in front of her eyes. "Had yourself quite a tumble there."

"I feel like a fool."

Aden had spent better than an hour on the roof of what was essentially a death trap and climbed down unscathed, yet she'd tripped on an old tree root and... Was she bleeding? Tilting her palms, she inspected the small cuts and scratches.

"You should put something on those." Aden's voice remained close to her ear, and he'd yet to let go of her arm.

"Yeah, well, that's what I get for being distracted."

"What were you thinking about?"

He sent her that annoying grin of his, and she groaned with irritation. They were in the middle of an emergency. He had nothing to grin about.

"I don't remember," she said. Like she'd tell him the truth. *Your hair.* "What time is it? We should probably head home. I need to feed the cattle. Make some calls." There were still several landowners on the route to Tumble Rock she hadn't reached.

When her phone rang with the tone identifying the ranch, she answered, grateful for the distraction. While Aden, her grandfather and Harlan engaged in conversation, she assured her distraught grandmother that they were leaving shortly. It had been a rough few days for all of them, and poor Grandma Sandy was feeling the strain. She promised to have coffee and the last of the pie waiting for them when they arrived home.

"Don't go to any trouble, Grandma."

"We either eat it up or feed it to Zip," she said.

"Are you sure you won't come with us?" Aden asked Harlan when they gathered by their trucks. "We have plenty of room."

"Nope." The older man scraped a lock of long silver hair off his face and readjusted the sunglasses he'd been wearing for eye protection while digging the firebreak. The purple, flowered sunglasses added to his already comical appearance. "I'm going to sit up on that roof there, have me a big glass of cold water and watch the fire."

"You hightail it inside like we discussed if the fire comes this way."

"I will, I will. Quit yer nagging. If I need to make a quick escape, I'll drive the ATV outta here. Follow the creek down the mountain and submerge myself in the fishing hole."

Rayna thought every part of his plan sounded totally insane.

Aden, too, given his expression. "Don't wait until the last second."

"I've got my radio," Harlan said. "I'll keep it tuned to the news."

"I'll stop by in the morning if I can. Just in case."

"Suit yourself."

Rayna insisted on driving the ranch pickup, and Grandpa Will didn't object. He wanted to ride with the young whippersnapper they'd hired to work for the summer. Rayna watched him get in Aden's truck, his movements slow and his eyes cloudy. Worry gnawed at her. He'd begun showing signs of disorientation and confusion again, which often happened when he was overtired.

Driving the ranch pickup alone, she followed closely behind Aden and her grandfather, her spirit every bit as weary as her aching muscles.

How was she ever going to accomplish everything? Protect her family and evacuate them. Safeguard the ranch. Drive the cattle to Tumble Rock. Sell them off, if necessary. What if she failed? Her grandparents could lose everything.

The enormity of what lay ahead bore down on her. Glad to be alone, she let the tears fall, wiping them away with an old tissue she found wedged in the seat. A moment later, she sucked in a gasp, stomped on the brake and stared at the glowing, almost unreal vision in the distance.

Through the gray, hazy atmosphere, she watched as the fire lit the entire tops of the mountains behind Happenstance. Black smoke poured from the flames, growing white as it rose skyward. A plane flew overhead, dropping chemicals that seemed to have no effect. Trucks and people scurried about at the base of the mountain, the firefighters identifiable by their bright yellow uniforms.

Rayna watched, transfixed. From this height and angle, the fire looked to be descending on the town, an unstoppable monster of pure fury. Fear turned every cell in her body to ice and despite the intense heat of the day her teeth began to chatter.

"No, no, no!"

Her mind told her this was merely an optical illusion. Her eyes playing tricks on her. The fire hadn't reached Happenstance and may bypass it completely.

Nonetheless, she couldn't shake the feeling that she was seeing a premonition of what could, and likely *would*, happen to her beloved town if the fire continued to burn uncontained.

She placed a hand over her heart and whispered, "Please, Lord. Still the winds. Bring the rain. Send help. Spare Happenstance. Grant me courage and show me what I need to do."

Feeling a tiny bit restored, she pulled ahead, accelerating to catch up with Aden and Grandpa Will.

Aden didn't remember hay being this heavy. Then again, he'd been a lot younger the last time he'd loaded hundred-pound bales onto a flatbed trailer. Fifty bales, to be exact. His arms and shoulders were tallying each one. As were his lungs. He'd been forced to stop more than once to rest.

The job wasn't just hard, it was also dirty and sweaty, made worse by the horrific air quality. The bandanna protected him from more than the thick smoke. Dust and debris surrounded him like a swarm of buzzing insects. Particles landed on his exposed skin, crawling inside his shirtsleeves and underneath his collar, where they caused intense itching and chafing.

Seized by a racking cough he couldn't suppress, he pressed his mouth into the crook of his elbow. Determined to power through, he continued when the cough subsided. So much for following doctor's orders and staying indoors. But he couldn't let down the Deweys. No way were they capable of feeding the cattle by themselves.

He stood atop an extension ladder that leaned against a tall tower of hay. Pulling off another bale, he flung it over the side. Ten more to go.

While grueling work, the hay would provide the cattle with extra energy they'd need for the long drive ahead. If Rayna wound up driving them to Tumble Rock in the morning—and as of now, she still planned to do so—the cattle needed a decent meal beforehand. There'd be little opportunity along the way to graze. While fifty bales wasn't enough to fully satisfy over two hundred head, it would supplement what grass remained in the pasture and was better than nothing.

He really wished Rayna would cut the cattle loose. While he understood her reasons, he disliked the odds. They weren't in her favor.

A groan of frustration escaped. What was he going to do about her and the Deweys? He'd been hoping for a clear sign from above as to his purpose here but hadn't yet been given one. At first, he thought it had been to find Will when the old man went missing. Except they'd found him easily enough and returned him home safely, helping to secure Harlan's home in the process—though Aden would rather the eccentric octogenarian had come with them. Hopefully, a deputy would stop by to check on Harlan and have better luck convincing him to evacuate.

Sandy had taken it for granted that Aden would spend a second night with them in their barn. Rayna, too. Then again, he'd promised her he'd stay. To be honest, a part of him was glad. Though he claimed to prefer solitude to companionship, she and the Deweys were fast becoming his favorite people. He had no business thinking about Rayna the way he had been these last twenty-four hours. They had no future prospects and never would once she learned the truth about his part in the market robbery.

But being near her made him feel good in a way he hadn't in a long time, possibly ever, and he wanted to enjoy that feeling a little longer before it inevitably ended.

His orders to remain in the area were also keeping him here. Was that God's purpose for him? Other ranchers besides the Deweys may require his help. Those who hadn't left already were expected to evacuate tomorrow. Aden had heard of another local besides Harlan, brave or foolhardy depending on opinion, refusing to abandon his home. The guy had sent his wife and kids away but remained behind, taking the chance that firefighters would contain the blaze in time or bypass his place altogether.

The thought of the fire ravaging homes Aden drove past daily sent a shudder through him. He took out his phone and set the alarm for both midnight and three a.m. He'd rest easier with periodic updates on the fire's location and estimated direction, assuming he got any rest at all. If necessary, Rayna and her family could embark on the cattle drive earlier than their scheduled dawn departure.

Grabbing another bale, the twine digging into the leather of his work gloves, he sent it sailing down to the ground. The bale hit with a muffled thud, releasing a cloud of dust and dirt before tumbling sideways to collide with the rest of the bales. Once Aden had all fifty on the ground, he climbed down the extension ladder.

At the bottom, he indulged in another brief rest. He'd just hefted the first bale onto the flatbed trailer when he heard barking. Zip bounded over from around the corner of the barn. Aden's pulse spiked. The dog's appearance could mean only one thing: Rayna was with him.

"Hey, boy."

Zip jumped up and planted his front paws on Aden's stomach. Throwing his head back, the dog yapped excitedly.

Rayna appeared and walked toward them, carrying a couple of water bottles. Aden appreciated Zip's excitement. He felt a fair amount of his own. Maybe not for the same reason. He ruffled the dog's ears.

"Zip. Get down," she scolded. "Aden, don't encourage him."

"All right, boy. Fun's over."

The dog twisted sideways and sped off, presumably on the hunt for more mischief.

Rayna fixed Aden with the impatient stare she usually reserved for Colton.

"What?" Aden asked, using his bandanna to wipe the sweat from his face.

"You were supposed to wait for help. You can't do—" she gestured to the cluster of bales "—all this by yourself."

"I just did."

"I would've helped." She passed him a bottled water.

"Can you lift a bale of hay on your own?"

"Yes." She straightened her spine.

"How many? One? Two?" He drained the entire bottle of water in several long swallows.

She evaluated the hay bales. "Well, not this many obviously. But I could have handled my share."

"You took care of your family. That's what mattered most. I don't mind grunt work."

"I'm stronger than you think."

"Show me." He reached for a bale, lifting it up and onto the trailer and setting it beside the first one.

"I will."

She extracted her own gloves from her back pocket, put them on and lifted a bale. Grunting softly, she wrestled with the bale until she finally had it on the trailer and tucked into place. The effort left her flushed and breathless.

"Well done." He chuckled and grabbed another bale. "You showed me up."

Aden gave her credit. She hadn't quit.

Together they finished, him loading six bales to her two. He didn't point that out.

"Grandma's fixing dinner," Rayna announced when they were done. Removing her gloves, she indulged in a long swallow of water.

"We just had pie an hour ago."

Sandy had made sure there was hot coffee and leftover pie when they'd returned from Harlan's. They'd eaten outside, everyone too filthy to be allowed in the house, according to Sandy.

"An hour and a half. And we're not eating dinner

till six. Late for us ranchers," Rayna said. She looked ready to collapse.

Aden removed his gloves, letting his sweat-drenched hands breathe, and sat on the back end of the flatbed. His lungs silently thanked him. "I talked to my supervisor a little while ago."

"Did you?" Rayna joined him on the trailer. "Any news? Beyond what you told us earlier?"

Aden glanced in the direction of the fire, which was straight north of town and about eight miles away. The distance seemed like a lot, but in terms of a forest fire it wasn't. Not if the wind picked up.

"Incident Command Post predicts the fire'll reach the outskirts of Happenstance by midmorning tomorrow if not contained."

"Is that possible? Containment?"

"We'd need a miracle."

Not for the first time, he was glad the Dewey ranch lay south of town. The family cabin and Harlan's property, however, were north of here and considerably closer to the fire.

"It's a good thing we're leaving at dawn," Rayna said soberly.

"I think you should reconsider. The cattle drive. It's a reckless plan."

"I get it. You disapprove." She turned away, the gesture speaking volumes.

Something inside Aden snapped. Without thinking, he rose and grabbed her hand. She drew back, more in surprise than alarm.

"Come on." He tugged her to her feet.

"Where are we going?"

"On a short trip."

"A trip? But what about the hay?"

"The cattle can wait. They have grass."

"Aden, I'm not going anywhere."

"There's something you need to see." He stopped midstep and met her gaze. "It's important, Rayna. We won't be gone long, I promise. Call your grandmother and let her know."

"Are you going to try and change my mind about the cattle drive?" she asked.

"I want you to fully understand the risks you're taking. If you go with me, I promise this will be the last time we talk about it."

He thought he might have to press harder. Instead, she acquiesced, calling Sandy as they piled into his truck and asking her to keep an eye on Colton. Zip insisted on coming along and rode in the back seat, his head hanging out the window and tongue lolling despite the smoke and heat and swirling ash.

They traveled a seldom-used lumber road. Initially, they passed no vehicles. Those evacuating Happenstance were taking the east road on the opposite side of town. Ahead of them, the fire blazed on the distant mountain, the smoke billowing skyward in enormous plumes. It was, Aden thought, strangely compelling and terribly beautiful.

As they drew nearer to the fire, they encountered one emergency and two service vehicles, coming and going. The drivers didn't motion Aden back, possibly because they recognized his forest service logo and assumed he was on ranger business.

He knew right where he was taking Rayna: Ezekiel's Hand. The remote spot was a regular stop for the Jeep tour company in town and a must-see for the more adventurous hikers. The overhang, with its unique rock formations, resembled a hand reaching out from the side of the mountain. The ledge faced the most western part of the valley and offered spectacular views in three directions. Today it would give Aden and Rayna an incredible bird's-eye view of the fire.

Apparently, Rayna had been here before. He should have figured as much—most everyone in Happenstance had visited the spot at some time in their life.

"Ezekiel's Hand," she said when he turned onto the rocky dirt road.

"Yeah."

The truck groaned as it made the ascent. Tall pine trees bracketed both sides of the road, the long limbs blocking the sky's dim gray light and turning afternoon into dusk. Half the needles on every tree were dark brown rather than lustrous green, casualties of the recent four-month drought. The sight, and the knowledge that the needles would burn away to nothing should the fire come this way, filled Aden with intense sadness.

All of a sudden, the road came to an abrupt stop, dead-ending when they encountered a forest service fence and gate.

"We walk from here," Aden said and led the way.

Zip trotted ahead of them, stopping now and then when a smell tempted him.

Rayna followed Aden, picking her way on the steep and narrow trail. "I've seen the view of the valley from here."

"Not during a wildfire, you haven't," he answered over his shoulder.

At the top of the incline, the heavy growth gradually gave way. Pushing aside a branch that poked at him with thorny fingers, he climbed out onto the overhang as if emerging from a cave into the open air—only to pause. Behind him, Rayna let out a gasp.

Directly across from them, the fire ravaged the mountain. Flames climbed along the top and down the side, releasing giant plumes of smoke that might have erupted from a volcano's mouth. In the wake of the flames lay hundreds of acres of blackened and smoldering earth dotted with minifires that could burn for days, even a week. Skeletons of trees, black as coal, stood like an army of the dead, their broken and twisted branches portraits of agony.

A distant crash echoed across the valley, causing Rayna to jump. In the next instant, a giant cloud of smoke and ash rose from where the scorched tree had fallen, its base and roots burned right out from beneath it.

A loud boom came next, emanating from the center of the fire. Zip stood on the overhang as if braced for an attack and barked a warning.

"Are they setting off dynamite?" Rayna asked.

"I don't see the firefighters in that area. My guess is it's a tree."

"A tree exploded?"

"It happens when the heat reaches three hundred degrees. Especially when trees are as dry as these ones."

"Dear Lord." She stared out across the expanse. "I hope no one was nearby."

"Rocks explode, too."

"That's possible?"

"At five hundred degrees." Aden lifted the binoculars he'd slung around his neck and scanned the area.

"Most of the firefighters seem to be below and ahead of the fire. Look." He pointed.

"I see them."

Emergency vehicles and fire trucks were parked in a line on the road at the base of the mountain and well below the fire. Halfway up, firefighters moved as one, identifiable by their protective gear and heavy equipment. As Aden and Rayna watched, one of the trucks pulled away, the hotshots hanging on to the sides as smoke swallowed all but their boots.

Through the binoculars, Aden spotted the yellow shirts of more hotshots in front of the fire.

"Here. Take a look." He handed the binoculars to Rayna, who put them to her face. "See those firefighters to the northwest?"

"What are they doing?"

"My guess is establishing a control line, trying to prevent the fire from encroaching on town. They could also be preparing for a back-burn. That's where they build a controlled fire to head off the wildfire."

"Sounds dangerous," Rayna said.

"It is. Very dangerous." Aden stopped to listen, tilting his head toward a distant *thup, thup, thup.* "Hear that?"

Zip resumed barking, this time at the sky.

"Is that a…"

Before Rayna could finish, a helicopter materialized overhead, flying so low they could read the numbers on the underside. It carried a giant bucket suspended from a cable that swung wide when the helicopter banked slowly left and then circled back toward the fire.

"Are they carrying fire retardant?" Rayna peered through the binoculars.

"Watch."

The helicopter flew just above the fire's reach, weaving in and out of the smoke. As if on cue, the bucket opened, and an enormous spray of water fell onto the heart of the fire. The flames danced, their centers almost white scarlet and their outsides shimmering orange. As if in agony, they writhed before shrinking in size.

"That's incredible!" Rayna lowered the binoculars and turned toward Aden, her green eyes alight with wonder and amazement.

Returning his attention to the helicopter required some effort. "Pretty impressive."

"Where did they get the water? I heard on the news water is scarce because of the drought, which is making fighting the fire more difficult."

"Some supply. Payson, maybe. Or Globe."

"Roosevelt Lake?"

"Too far. Could be getting the water from swimming pools. Big ones, like at the resort or the Payson city park."

"How? Do they drop the bucket in the pool?"

"Something like that. Skim the bucket across the water like you'd fill a pail."

"Water from a pool," she repeated in disbelief.

"Whatever it takes. There are limited natural resources available right now."

Having emptied its bucket, the helicopter came around and headed back the way it had come, flying higher. Perhaps because its load was lighter.

Another tree collapsed, this one rolling a good twenty yards before slowing to a stop. For a few seconds, both Aden and Rayna simply stared.

After a moment, he said, "Next to a nuclear explosion, there's no killing force more lethal than a big forest fire."

"Is that really true?" she asked in a stunned voice.

"So I've been told." He pointed again, this time to the east. "See those white tents and trailers way over there in the valley floor below Saurus Mountain?"

"Yeah."

"That's Incident Command Post. The tent with the ambulances parked out front is the field hospital."

"Where you were taken after your smoke inhalation?"

He nodded.

"Are the other ones for housing?"

"That. A dining hall. Equipment storage."

They watched together in silence for several minutes. Aden could see from Rayna's expression the difficulty she had taking it all in. Good. That had been his intention. She should know the acute seriousness of the situation.

"Ready to go?" he eventually asked.

She continued staring. "I had no idea. I hear the news and people talking. But you really don't know. Not until you see for yourself."

"This fire means business, Rayna. All those firefighters down there, all that equipment and those vehicles, will be next to useless to save the town if the weather conspires against us. You and your family have to leave."

"I know."

"I'll help with anything you need. But saving your family is what's most important."

He led the way back to the truck. She barely spoke until she climbed into the cab.

"If you were hoping to discourage me, you didn't."

"It was worth a shot."

"Even if my grandparents' entire savings wasn't tied up in the cattle, there's no way I could leave them behind to face that fire. They wouldn't survive. During the Yavapai Fire, some ranchers lost thirty to fifty percent of their herd." She straightened her spine. "I won't be responsible for causing the agonizing deaths of my grandparents' cattle. Not when there's a chance I can save them."

"Well, then." Aden started the truck. "You'd better figure out how you're going to manage the drive with two old people, a kid and a dog. Because you don't have much time."

Chapter Six

Rayna observed Aden from the corner of her eye during the drive home from Ezekiel's Hand. He'd been unusually quiet even for him. Then again, she'd been quiet, too. She doubted he was happy with her. He'd hoped to discourage her from driving the cattle to Tumble Rock, and all he'd done was increase her conviction that she was doing the right thing. The *only possible* thing.

Rather than park his truck behind the house per usual—when did he start having a usual spot?—he continued to the barn, where he pulled in alongside the flatbed trailer loaded with hay.

He looked at her when she didn't immediately move. "We'd better get these cattle fed."

She nodded, a part of her still processing the scenes from the fire. It was far enough away she didn't fear for the ranch. The family cabin and Harlan's place were a different story. They were much closer.

Zip launched himself out of the truck the instant she opened the rear door, and ran in circles, barking. It was like he'd understood what Aden had said and was ready to work.

They got right to the—in Aden's case—backbreaking and grimy chore. Rayna had the easy part. She drove the truck and trailer while he walked beside it, dragging off a bale about every twenty feet and dropping it onto the ground. He cut the bale open with his multitool, letting the hay split apart into sections. He then wound the strands of twine into a small cluster, knotted it and tossed it onto the flatbed. From the rearview mirror, Rayna watched as a large pile accumulated.

The cattle meandered from all corners of the large pasture, following in the wake of the truck and trailer. Bellowing, snorting and grunting, they competed for the choicest feeding spots. Zip darted to and fro, herding them over. It wasn't necessary. The hungry cattle needed no enticement. By the time Rayna and Aden finished, the line of hay and grazing cattle stretched across half the pasture.

Aden climbed into the pickup beside her for the return drive to the barn. Zip hopped onto the flatbed, barking at another helicopter flying overhead. It traveled in a straight line away from them, leaving the dense gray smoke directly above them and entering a sea of bright orange.

Not the sun, rather the fire's reflection. It lit the entire northwestern sky from one end to the other. Rayna had never seen anything like it.

Once Aden was settled, she pulled forward, the silence from earlier resuming. Which was why his remark when they arrived back at the barn came unexpectedly.

"There's another option, Rayna," he said as she maneuvered the flatbed trailer into its parking slot beside the haystacks. "Other than driving the cattle to Tumble Rock."

"You said if I went with you to look at the fire you wouldn't bring up the cattle again."

"Hear me out. I've been thinking."

"Okay, I'm listening."

They got out of the truck and went around to the back where she watched Aden unhitch the trailer. He bent over the jack and vigorously turned the crank, removing the coupling from the ball at the right moment. She kicked the wooden block over and he rested the trailer hitch on it.

"What if we built a firebreak around the pastures," he continued. "Like what we did at Harlan's house only bigger and wider."

"That's a significant undertaking," Rayna insisted. "I doubt we'd have time."

"We could work all night."

"We have a better chance of saving the cattle if we drive them to Tumble Rock."

"Consider the idea for just a moment."

"How will the cattle know they're supposed to stay inside the firebreak? Won't they panic and run?"

"They might." He straightened.

"Are we supposed to remain here and watch them?"

"No."

She didn't like the idea. "In other words, we take our chances that the cattle will survive."

"You and your family will be safe."

"And potentially flat broke."

"What are the other ranchers doing?" he asked, fastening the safety chain. "Have you talked to them?"

"Some are waiting for an update. Some leaving. Some staying behind to protect their livestock. But you know that already, don't you?"

He didn't answer her, maybe because she was right.

"Pastor Leonard called me while we were feeding the cattle," she said. "He found a volunteer willing to help us drive the cattle."

"Who?"

"Claire Weatherby."

Aden glanced away. She almost hadn't told him for this very reason. She'd known how he'd respond.

"She's very experienced," Rayna insisted. "She and her late husband had a ranch for thirty years, and she participated in a dozen of the commemorative cattle drives."

"She's in her sixties."

"Early sixties and very fit for her age."

She could see him reining in his impatience. At least, he tried to rein it in. When he spoke, his tone took on a sharp edge.

"You're seriously planning on driving over two hundred head of cattle along twenty miles of back roads, most of those not regularly maintained, with only yourself, your elderly grandparents and Claire Weatherby?"

"Don't forget Zip. He's as good a herder as any person. That's five. I can drive the cattle with five."

They both looked at the dog, who pounced on a crawling beetle and then tried to eat it.

"Four and a half," Aden said.

"With you I'd have six." Rayna hadn't intended for that to slip out, it just had.

"I can't. I have to work. Help the firefighters. They need all the manpower they can muster."

"You haven't been medically cleared."

"I should be tomorrow. And if I'm not, I'll assist with the evacuation. Town officials have formed a center at the high school gym for people needing supplies and rides."

"You said you'd stay," she whispered.

"To see you and your family evacuated. And I will." His voice gentled. "I didn't promise to come on the drive with you."

She hadn't realized how much she wanted him to accompany them until that moment. The determination that had been fueling her resolve slowly seeped away.

"I'm sorry," she said. "I have no right making demands. You've done more than enough already and don't owe us a thing."

"I do owe you. For what happened to your grandfather during the assault."

"You're not responsible for your brother's actions."

He worked his jaw as if considering saying more but didn't.

"Don't worry. We'll manage," she said when he remained quiet.

"I worry about you." His gaze roamed her face as if studying every nuance.

Rayna almost imagined him saying, *I* care *about you.*

She instantly chided herself. There was nothing between them. He was simply repaying what he perceived as a debt to her grandparents. Thinking there might be more was ridiculous.

The clanging dinner bell interrupted them. Good. Rayna had no desire to continue their conversation and made sure to maintain her distance from him on the walk back to the house.

They washed up with the garden hose, including Zip's paws—something Grandma Sandy insisted on before they came inside to eat. Rayna half expected

Aden to request a meal-to-go and head for the barn. Again, he surprised her and sat at the kitchen table, appearing quite comfortable with her family.

Talk during the meal centered on preparedness for leaving at dawn, the rigors of the cattle drive and the prayer vigil starting at eight tonight. Someone from church had phoned Grandma Sandy while she was fixing dinner to inform her of the community effort, and she'd insisted they all take part. All except Aden. Him, she'd invited. Then she'd broken into a wide grin when he'd accepted.

Rayna took that to mean Aden would for certain be spending the night again. The fresh towels Grandma Sandy had placed in the hall bathroom were another indicator. "For your shower," she'd told him.

Wasn't that what she wanted? Rayna asked herself. For Aden to stay and help them prepare to evacuate? If yes, then why wasn't she happier?

The answer came in the form of a small niggling voice. *Because he's staying out of an obligation to your family, not for you.*

These changes in her feelings toward Aden were baffling. Rayna didn't believe herself capable of caring for another man. Steven had been, still was, her soul mate. The love of her life. There was no room in her heart for someone new.

But even as she watched Aden interact with her family—listen intently to Grandpa Will's story, compliment Grandma Sandy on her cooking and joke with Colton—she experienced a slight shift. He'd surprised her, and she hadn't thought that would happen again, either.

"Let's have coffee and dessert on the front porch,"

Grandma Sandy announced. "I took a carrot cake out of the freezer. Your favorite, Will. We can watch the fire before the prayer vigil at eight."

"I don't like carrots," Colton complained.

"You'll like these, young man. Guaranteed." Grandpa Will tweaked Colton's nose and then gave Grandma Sandy a hand with cutting and serving the cake.

"Do I get to stay up late?" Colton asked.

"No, sweetie." Rayna fetched forks and napkins to carry outside. "We have to wake early tomorrow." Leave it to her son to try and turn every situation around to his advantage.

As she strolled through the living room, she noticed the preparations her grandmother had made for the prayer vigil.

"I was thinking," Grandma Sandy said, taking a seat in one of the wooden rockers on the porch. "We could each say a prayer out loud. If you're comfortable with that." Her gaze went to Aden, who, along with the others, had found a place to sit.

He nodded. His gentle smile in response to her grandmother's inquiry wound its way into Rayna's heart and found an empty spot to reside. Seemed she was wrong. She did have room, after all.

"Wonderful," Grandma Sandy gushed.

The next second, Aden's phone vibrated from his pocket. Everyone stopped eating to stare at him expectantly. He read the display, his brows drawing together.

"If you'll excuse me. I need to take this. It's my supervisor." He got up from his chair, answering the phone as he headed back inside. "Yeah, Tom…No, not a problem." He shut the door behind him.

He might have taken all the sound with him, for a hush descended on the group.

"What do you think that's about?" Grandma Sandy eventually asked.

"He'll tell us if we need to know," Grandpa Will grumbled.

Rayna lost all interest in her cake, her stomach shrinking to the size of a golf ball.

"It's ranger business," Colton announced, relieving some of the tension.

They picked at their cake until Aden returned five minutes later, pocketing his phone. Rayna swore they all expelled a collective sigh of relief.

"Sorry about that," he said and resumed his seat.

"Any news?" Grandma Sandy asked with a forced casualness that fooled no one.

"Yes." He pushed his cake around on the plate rather than eat. The call must have upset him.

"Uh-oh." Grandma Sandy set her fork down. "That doesn't bode well."

"The fire's reached the McCullough homestead."

"What! Oh dear, oh dear," Grandma Sandy said, her eyes widening. And hers weren't the only ones.

Rayna swallowed a gasp. "When?" she asked.

"An hour ago."

"That's terrible." Grandma Sandy's shoulders caved inward as if she'd been punched in the chest. "I can't believe it."

"A real shame," Grandpa Will added.

"Is everything lost?" Rayna asked, a hitch in her voice.

Aden's expression remained solemn. "The foundation and chimney are all that's left of the house. A few charred columns in what was the barn are still standing."

She closed her eyes. Any loss of property was a tragedy. The homestead, however, was a significant piece of Happenstance's colorful history. It, along with a small museum in town, was dedicated to the bloody feud that had occurred there. Both the homestead and the museum contributed to the town's economy by bringing tourists and historians. Scenes from a movie had once been filmed there.

"What's a culla home?" Colton asked.

"We visited there once. Last year. Maybe you were too young to remember." Rayna wished she'd taken Colton more recently. Now he'd never get to enjoy the iconic landmark.

The McCulloughs had been among the area's more prominent settlers in the early 1900s. They'd brought sheep to the valley, a move that had triggered a violent feud between them and their cattle-owning neighbors, the Franklins. The feud had ended in a battle with both sides sustaining grievous injuries and multiple deaths. The Franklins were ultimately declared the victors, more likely a political move than anything else as cattle brought in far more money to the valley than sheep did.

"The fire is really coming, isn't it?" Rayna asked, setting her unfinished cake on a side table.

"The wind hasn't changed direction yet," Aden said. "As of right now, it's still driving the fire mostly south. That could and likely will change. The question is when. If the fire remains restricted to the outskirts or continues straight south, Happenstance proper will be safe. Firebreaks are being constructed as we speak. Nonetheless, ranches and vacation homes on the outskirts are bound to fall victim. My big concern is the town dump."

"Dear Lord." Grandma Sandy pressed a crumpled napkin to her mouth.

Grandpa Will shook his head. "That dump's gonna burn something awful, what with all the trash."

"Worse than that," Aden said. "It's full of accelerants, and that'll increase the fire's spread exponentially."

"What does that mean?" Colton asked.

"It's bad news," Grandpa Will said.

Aden also left the remainder of his cake untouched. Like Rayna, he'd clearly lost his appetite. "You may not want to wait until morning to evacuate."

"What does your supervisor say?"

"He thinks everyone should be gone already."

Everyone should be gone already, Rayna thought. Not *we* should be gone. Aden wasn't including himself.

"Not before our prayer vigil," Grandma insisted.

"We can't drive the cattle at night, anyway," Rayna cut in. "We have to wait until morning when it's light. Near morning at least."

"Rayna," Aden began.

"We've been through this. More than once. I'm not cutting the cattle loose. And neither are we building a firebreak. We're driving them to Tumble Rock," she said decisively. "I already called Claire. She's meeting us here in the morning."

"Then, I think, you'd better pray hard during the vigil tonight." He rose and carried his plate and fork inside.

Rayna stared after him, sensing the eyes of her grandmother boring into her. Whether in annoyance or curiosity, she wasn't sure.

* * *

By eight p.m. sharp, Aden and the Deweys had gathered in the living room. Sandy had cleared the coffee table, moving the knickknacks and a pair of candlesticks to the dining room. Aden couldn't help thinking a campfire ignited by a single flame no bigger than one on a candle had set in motion a disaster that would affect the town and its people for decades to come.

Sandy, Will and Rayna perched side by side on the couch while Colton occupied the floor, more interested in getting Zip to shake a paw than anything else. Aden chose the wingback chair in the corner. He was pretty sure he'd sat in this same chair the summer he'd worked here. Zip sat in the middle of the room, observing the goings-on with keen interest.

"I'll start," Sandy said and took Will's gnarled hand in hers. She closed her eyes and drew in a deep breath. "Be merciful unto me, O God, be merciful unto me: for my soul trusteth in Thee: yea, in the shadow of Thy wings will I make my refuge, until these calamities be overpast."

Aden recognized the opening lines from Psalm 57 and thought Sandy couldn't have picked a more appropriate way to begin the prayer vigil.

"We ask for Your protection during this perilous and scary time," she continued. "Watch over us as we make our difficult journey tomorrow. Give us strength and courage to face the challenges that lie ahead. Guide our way with Your loving light. Safeguard the people of Happenstance on their travels as they evacuate. Keep them and their homes clear of the fire's path. Bless the brave individuals who are fighting the fire and the volunteers assisting those in need. Return them uninjured into the arms of their families. Give speed to the precious wildlife fleeing the fire and lead them to sanctuary."

Aden also closed his eyes as he listened, letting Sandy's words soothe his spirit and untangle his thoughts. In his mind, he recalled Pastor Leonard reciting one of his many lessons and truly hearing the word of God for the first time. It was one of many days that had changed Aden's life. And while he couldn't explain why, something told him tomorrow would be another one.

Sandy ended her prayer by thanking God for sending Aden to them. When Will's turn came, he asked that Harlan and the family cabin be spared before losing his concentration and faltering. Colton prayed for God to take care of Zip and then threw his arms around the dog, squeezing his neck. Rayna asked for no problems on the cattle drive and for the fire to bypass the town.

When Aden's turn came, he took a moment to compose himself before speaking. He prayed regularly but never out loud in front of others. Sensing the stares of everyone in the room, he swallowed, cleared his mind and then let the words come of their own accord.

"Dear Lord. Rayna is Your good and faithful follower. Give her the fortitude and wisdom she needs to lead her family and the cattle to Tumble Rock. She's taken on a great responsibility, a monumental task. She needs Your strength to carry her, Your love to lift her and Your sage counsel to show her the way. In Jesus's name we pray. Amen."

A soft chorus of *amen*s followed. After a short period of silent reflection, Sandy excused herself and Will, claiming it was past their bedtime.

"These old bones of ours need some rest before the big day."

"Same for you, sweetie. Bedtime." Rayna collected a reluctant Colton and dragged him upstairs.

Left alone—well, not entirely alone, Zip had stayed—Aden returned to the front porch. He knew he should also head off to bed; four a.m. came mighty early. But he craved another few minutes of solitude. The prayer vigil had both replenished him and left a hollow ache in the center of his chest. He wished there was more he could do. For Rayna, her family and everyone in Happenstance. What purpose did God have for him? Aden still wasn't sure. Unless he went on the cattle drive with Rayna and the Deweys, his work here was done.

From his seat on the porch swing, he had an unrestricted view of the distant fire. Beneath the bright red and golden glow of the flames, the mountains had turned a shade of black darker than pitch. Planes and helicopters had ceased flying overhead, the risk of crashing too great at night. Although Aden couldn't see the hotshots and ground crews from here, he knew they continued to toil. The fire hadn't stopped burning merely because the sun had set. It waited for nothing and no one.

At the sound of the front door opening, he turned, surprised to see Rayna step outside. She hadn't seemed eager for his continued company, and he'd assumed she'd retired like everyone else.

"I saw you through the window." She lowered herself onto the swing beside him.

She must not be too angry at him or she would have

chosen the rocker on the other side of the porch, not sat right next to him. He admitting to liking her proximity.

"I wanted one last look at the fire."

She nodded and remained silent as if contemplating his remark. He let her mull—he was getting used to these long stretches of silence between them. At least this one wasn't riddled with tension.

"Thank you for your prayer earlier," she said.

"I figured you can use all the help you can get."

She smiled softly, the glow of the far-off fire turning her complexion a delicate golden hue. Another irony, he supposed, that something terrible could look beautiful when viewed from a different angle. Like before, she reminded Aden of the teenage girl she'd been when he'd worked for her grandparents. He felt the same pull of attraction now as he had then.

"When Steven was killed," Rayna finally said, meeting his gaze, "I felt utterly helpless. There was nothing I could have done to stop what happened, nothing I *could do* to change my and Colton's circumstances and nothing to make sure Steven got the justice he deserved. When the man who shot him struck a plea bargain with the prosecutor and received a reduced sentence in exchange for testifying in another case, I begged the judge at his sentencing hearing to be less lenient. It made no difference." She sniffed and blinked back tears. "Events spiraled out of my control, and all I could do was stand by and watch."

"I'm sorry, Rayna. That must have been awful."

"I swore then I would never be a powerless victim again. That I would fight for myself and my family with every fiber of my being and every resource at my disposal." She drew a shaky breath. "I'm not being stubborn, Aden. I'm taking charge of my life and refusing to let fate, or others, rob me of what's important again."

"I understand."

"Do you?" she asked.

"Not that I've lost a loved one, but until I ventured out on my own, I had no control over what happened to me."

"Because of *your* family?"

"If I resisted or refused…let's just say my parents didn't spare the rod."

Like praying out loud, Aden rarely shared the details of the life he'd led before finding God. People had a tendency to judge, they couldn't help themselves, and he'd grown weary of their scorn. Opening up to Rayna, however, felt different. She may have once held negative opinions of him, but the acceptance he now saw in her expression enabled him to speak freely.

"I was expected to be a contributing member of the Whitley household. First and foremost, scam the government or employers out of money. Disability, food stamps, welfare, workmen's comp, you name it. In a pinch, panhandle. Borrow money whenever possible, and under no circumstances repay it. Shoplift if the opportunity presented itself. Loaf off rather than earn an honest dollar. Always take the easy way out. Bully. Argue. Intimidate. Harass. Never back down. Never yield. And rule number one, family above all others and all things."

"You must have known what you were doing was wrong."

"Wrong legally? Of course. Stealing is against the law. So is spray-painting a building and taking the neighbor's car for a joyride without their permission.

But wrong morally? That's where things got a little muddy. My parents raised me and my brother to believe a different set of rules applied to us. When I landed in the principal's office for fighting, I was standing up for myself. When I bullied another kid or backtalked someone in authority, I was exercising my rights. When I vandalized or trespassed, I was simply having a little fun."

"And when you stole?"

"I was taking what I was entitled to. They had more than they needed, anyway." Shame roughened his voice, and he cleared his throat. "I was messed up. Still am."

"I don't buy that." Rayna stared at him. "If that good and decent man wasn't always there deep down inside, you wouldn't have changed. You'd have turned a deaf ear to Pastor Leonard and your back on God. Instead, you embraced them."

Aden smiled at a rush of memories. "Pastor Leonard took me camping with the youth group. Lived all my life in Happenstance, and that was the first time I slept outside. The first time I went fishing and hiking. It's true, I swear. He showed me a whole new world I had no idea existed. When I graduated high school, he helped me enroll in community college, find a part-time job and a room to rent. Higher education, gainful employment and independence. Something else the Whitleys were against. I transferred to Northern Arizona University, where I earned my degree in Parks and Recreation Management."

"I'm impressed."

"I admit, I surprised myself. Didn't think I'd stick with it. My family sure didn't. Their being convinced I'd fail motivated me more than anything else."

"Pastor Leonard must be very proud of you."

Aden lifted a shoulder. "He's the only one. The majority of folk in town believe I cheated my way through college."

"They might not if you stopped pushing them away."

She shifted closer as if to prove her point. Only an inch or two, but enough that Aden noticed. How could he not? He wasn't made of stone.

"I'm, um, a little lacking when it comes to people skills."

"Let them see the real you. They'll change their opinion. Like I have."

She lifted her hand and sifted her fingers through the hair on the side of his head. For an instant, he stiffened. Then, as she continued, he let himself relax, lulled by the sweet, gentle sensation of her touch.

"What are you doing, Rayna?" he asked, knowing that letting her continue was a mistake but not stopping her.

"Testing the waters."

"And?"

"I need more research."

She brought her face close and pressed her lips against his. Aden didn't dare move. He was too afraid she might pull away and end the magical moment.

"How about that?" Her eyes softened, and her voice lowered. "Something I would have sworn an impossibility just happened. Will wonders never cease?"

Aden longed to test the waters further. With a strength he didn't realize he possessed, he sat back.

"Oh." Rayna withdrew, her features crestfallen. "Sorry. I misread the signals."

"You didn't misread any signals." He took her hand

in his, more comfortable on this safer ground. "But I have to be honest with you."

"Okay."

"I like you. A lot. And I've thought of nothing but kissing you since I found you on the mountain with that cow and calf."

"What's wrong, then?"

He hesitated, well aware he was stalling and afraid she'd refuse to talk to him again once he revealed his secret.

"Aden?"

"You need to know. I did help my brother, Garret, the night of the robbery and assault. It's my fault your grandfather was hurt."

"I see."

"I was hiding behind the dumpster and supposed to warn Garret if anyone showed. When your grandfather pulled into the parking lot, I should have run out and told him Garret was inside. Only I didn't. Instead, I got scared and ran off. I've regretted my actions ever since."

To his surprise, she didn't turn away from him.

"I've suspected all along you were involved in the robbery."

She did? Then how could she have kissed him? "You have every right to hate me."

"I don't. Far from it. Like I said earlier, you're not that person anymore. You were young and forced into a bad situation by your brother. What he asked of you was unfair and unconscionable."

"Your grandpa was kind to me, and I didn't return his kindness. What kind of person does that make me?"

"Someone who made a mistake, regrets it, learned from it and now lives a Christian life. What kind of person would I be if I didn't understand and forgive?" She squeezed his fingers. "I like you, too, by the way."

"Rayna." He paused. "I don't…"

"What? Afraid I'll get my hopes up?" she asked. "I get there'll be challenges."

"I'm not good at relationships." The admission wasn't easy for him. "I haven't had a lot of practice, and I worry I'll disappoint you. Or start something I can't finish."

"I haven't had a lot of practice, either, other than Steven." She placed a hand on Aden's arm. "We can learn together."

"It's not that simple. You were married to a great guy, and I'm nothing like him. I live a very solitary life. I avoid socializing. My work isolates me. That's probably why people in town still don't trust me. And maybe they shouldn't."

"I don't care what other people think."

"Be sensible, Rayna. You have enough going on in your life without adding more problems. The ranch. Your grandparents. Colton. What if I disappoint them?" *Again*, when it came to Sandy and Will. "You need to put your family first. Especially now."

She nodded. "You're right. And I will. But, God willing, this fire will be contained soon, and the cattle herded to safety. Our lives will return to normal. Then you and I can see where our feelings lead us."

"That's just it. The situation is intense right now. So are our emotions. They could, and probably will, change once the danger passes."

"I don't believe that, but I understand your hesitancy."

"I'm not sure you do."

"You're trying to protect me from getting hurt."

He was. And himself, as well. "Let's just wait. Talk again in a few weeks."

"All right," she agreed and surprised him with a brief kiss before standing and returning to the house.

Aden remained sitting for a long while, replaying the last five minutes over and over. He had no doubt Rayna would eventually come to her senses and realize she could do a whole lot better than him. And when she did, they could go their separate ways. No harm, no foul.

Except he wouldn't get over her. Not for a long, long time. If ever.

Chapter Seven

Rayna filled the coffeemaker with water, pressed the brew button and waited for the familiar gurgling sound. While the pot filled, she conducted a final inspection of the refrigerator's contents. Good. Nothing left that would spoil during the next week. And if the fire reduced the house to a pile of smoldering ashes, what did it matter whether a block of cheese had grown moldy.

She pushed the thought from her mind, refusing to consider the possibility The house would be fine. Her family, too. She'd get them and the cattle safely to Tumble Rock and then return when the fire was contained to find the ranch intact and the town unscathed.

One devastating loss in her life was enough. There wouldn't be another one. She believed that, and she'd rely on her belief to see her through the days ahead.

She poured herself a cup of coffee, letting the steaming beverage revive her. She'd barely slept last night. Her mind had flitted from one worry to the next, thoughts of Aden weaving in and out. She'd kissed him! And it had been amazing.

A small flash of guilt had snuck up on her at around

midnight. She'd loved Steven to distraction. Would always love him. Had she been disloyal to him by kissing another?

Aden had a valid point. Perhaps no one would ever replace her late husband.

Her head argued no, that Steven wouldn't expect her to live the rest of her life alone. He'd want her to find someone who made her happy. Also someone who would be a good stepfather to Colton. Her heart required further convincing, however.

And besides, she was getting way ahead of herself, as Aden had warned her. They may not be right for each other and might see each other differently once the threat of the fire had passed. The fact was, she hardly knew him. Except he was the first man to give her butterflies since Steven.

Putting herself out there and making the first move hadn't been easy. She wouldn't have thought herself capable of it as recently as yesterday morning. Almost with each passing hour, Aden revealed something new about himself that caused her to feel differently about him *and* about herself. She'd also assumed just because she was ready to consider a romantic relationship, Aden was, too. Their mutual attraction was real, that much was certain. But that might be all it was.

When he'd admitted his part in the robbery and assault, she honestly hadn't cared. He wasn't the same person now as then, and the troubled youth had matured into a fine and caring man who couldn't be more different from the rest of his family. She wouldn't have kissed him otherwise.

Whatever happened to them, he really needed to get the Whitleys out of his head and stop allowing them—and what he'd convinced himself others thought of him—to dictate his life. The changes he'd made, the help he gave others, the love he poured into his job, should be more than enough to erase the bad and make him worthy of any woman's love and any person's friendship.

When this crisis was over and they'd returned home, maybe she could find a way to open people's eyes and hearts to Aden. He deserved as much for all he did even if—she didn't want to think this—things didn't work out for them. He'd risked his own health searching for her grandfather and securing Harlan's property, and he deserved her support.

Taking another sip of coffee, Rayna noted the time— 4:10, according to the clock on the stove. She hadn't woken Colton yet, deciding to let him sleep until the last minute. Zip, too, who snoozed at the foot of Colton's bed. The dog had a long day ahead of him and needed his rest. They all did.

Upstairs, she heard her grandparents padding about. A closet door closed. Pipes in the wall groaned and creaked as water rushed through them. Muffled voices alternately rose and fell in volume.

Rayna sat at the kitchen table and mentally reviewed her long list, going over each item. Gather the chickens and put them into crates. Trap the barn cats and wrangle them into the pet carrier. Load the crates with the chickens, the carrier with cats and the two goats into the horse trailer. She'd ride Bisbee and tie the other two horses to the side of the trailer. They'd have to walk alongside for the duration of the cattle drive. Their extra weight would make the trailer too heavy for the rougher spots along the roads and potentially cause them to get stuck.

Aden's words about cutting the livestock loose replayed in her head. Not happening. She wouldn't leave any of the cattle behind. Hoping they were smart enough to stay within the firebreak or outrun the flames wasn't enough for Rayna. She'd seen pictures of scorched and burned livestock, victims of wildfires. The cattle may not like the long and tiring drive, but it beat the alternative.

She continued reviewing her mental list. Bins with food and clothes and necessities would go in the truck bed, along with the camping equipment. They'd need at least a dozen bales of hay, too, in order to lure the cattle at the start of the drive and possibly later at the Overbecks' ranch. Once the first cows were enticed to follow the truck and trailer, the rest would come with only minimal coaxing. That was the good thing about herd animals, their instincts were to stay together in a tightly clustered group.

Grandma Sandy would drive the truck and lead the herd, Grandpa and Colton her passengers. It was a big responsibility, and Rayna worried her grandmother might not be up to the task. Claire Weatherby would ride her horse midherd. She'd texted Rayna a little bit ago confirming she'd meet them at the pastures in an hour. Rayna and Zip would bring up the rear and keep watch for any stragglers.

Dense smoke had begun interfering with cell phone reception. Rayna had instructed her grandma and Claire to not wait for trouble and call each other whenever they had a decent signal.

For the third time since she'd come into the kitchen,

Rayna checked for a missed text or call from Pastor Leonard. Nothing. Maybe he'd been able to find one more person to come on the cattle drive and was waiting until a decent hour to contact her. She resisted admitting even to herself that she hoped Aden would change his mind and go with them. But he'd been clear. Work came first, and he had every intention of returning to assist the firefighters or Search and Rescue the instant he was medically cleared.

She respected his devotion to duty. And after scaring him off last night with her kiss, there was no way he'd forgo his job to join them. The way he kept to himself, she might not see much of him after today. The possibility left a vague sense of…all right, she'd admit it. Disappointment.

Reaching for the map he'd drawn, she studied it yet again. If all went well, they'd make Tumble Rock in one day. One *very long* day. Depending on conditions of the back roads and any vehicles they encountered, the cattle would move at a pace of about two miles an hour. Cows weren't particularly fast. If they started the drive at 6 a.m. and continued straight through, they'd reach the Overbecks' sometime late afternoon.

Stopping along the way presented too many problems to be an option, including keeping the herd together and getting them moving again. The last two miles would be the trickiest as they had to take the main road—the only available route to reach the Overbeck ranch. Thank goodness the Overbecks were meeting them at the junction and had offered to stop traffic.

Noise from upstairs had quieted. Rayna assumed her grandparents were dressing. As she continued studying the map, a soft knock sounded on the back door.

She stood, a thrill winding through her when she recognized Aden's shadowy form through the kitchen-door window.

Ordering herself to relax, she let him in, smiling with an enthusiasm meant to convey she had no regrets about their kiss. "Morning."

He returned her smile, albeit with less enthusiasm. She sighed. There he went again, overthinking things.

"I saw the light on. Figured you were up." He stepped over the threshold, removing his cowboy hat as he did.

"Coffee's ready, if you want some."

"I could use about a gallon."

As he advanced into the light, she was taken aback by his appearance. Granted, she'd been awake much of the night. Aden, however, clearly hadn't slept a wink. Lines of fatigue bracketed his eyes, emphasizing his haggard expression. His rumpled hair defied his hand's attempt to smooth it, and his steps lacked their usual energy.

"Are you okay, Aden?" She fetched him a mug from the cupboard beside the sink. Was their kiss responsible?

"The level three evacuation order was issued thirty minutes ago. The fire's headed toward Happenstance's northwestern perimeter. It's moving really fast and will be there by midmorning."

While expected, the news knocked Rayna for a loop. "You heading to town now?"

"As soon as you've finished loading the truck and start on the drive."

She noticed that he was in uniform again. Grandma Sandy had washed his shirt and pants sometime yesterday. Interestingly, his demeanor had changed along with his clothes. He was once again the all-business forest ranger she'd first encountered.

"What about your medical clearance?" she asked.

"I'll stop first at the mobile hospital. I don't anticipate a problem."

She hadn't noticed him coughing anymore, but his lungs might not be fully healed. "Are you sure? Smoke inhalation is serious stuff."

"I feel fine."

"Do you think the cabin and Harlan's place are in danger?" All her questions. One might think she was trying to coerce him into staying.

"Yes. They're much closer to the projected path of the fire. A sheriff's deputy went by Harlan's late yesterday. He was still insisting on staying."

She closed her eyes, willing the old recluse to be sensible and change his mind. "Is there anything you can do?"

"If I can, I'll run by. No guarantees. My guess is they'll put me back to work on building firebreaks."

Rayna tried to smile, but her mouth refused. "I prayed that we'd wake up this morning and learn the winds had changed direction again or that the fire was contained."

Aden set down his half-drunk coffee on the counter. "I know I said I wouldn't bring it up again, but I wish you'd reconsider driving the cattle to Tumble Rock. If one thing goes wrong, if the winds pick up speed or the fire alters course, you and your family and all those cattle could be trapped."

"We're going southeast, in the opposite direction of the fire."

"If any of the cattle break loose, promise me you won't go after them."

"We'll see."

"Rayna. Losing a few cattle isn't worth the risk."

The ranch phone suddenly rang, giving her a start. "Maybe that's Pastor Leonard telling me he found a volunteer." She answered the ancient wall phone with a bright "Hello."

"Is this the Dewey residence?"

"Yes." At the man's serious tone, her pulse raced.

"I'm calling from the Gila County Sheriff's Office. Be advised a level three evacuation order has been issued for your area. You need to leave immediately."

"Yes. I just found out. We'll be on our way shortly."

"Don't delay."

He reviewed a few important evacuation details before ending the call, sounding eager to contact the next resident on his list. "Stay safe, ma'am."

"Thank you."

"Not Pastor Leonard, I take it," Aden said when she hung up.

"No. That was the sheriff's office."

"Rayna. About the cattle drive—"

She cut him off. "I need to wake up Colton."

"I'll help you finish packing."

"That isn't necessary."

"I want to."

"Okay." She relented only because she knew he wouldn't take no for an answer.

"About last night…"

"Don't say you wish it hadn't happened, because I don't."

"Me, either." He wrapped one of her curls around his finger. "But we have a lot to resolve."

Before she could respond, Grandma Sandy and Grandpa Will dragged into the kitchen. They clearly hadn't slept well, either. Colton and Zip seemed to be the only ones getting some decent shut-eye.

"Are we interrupting?" Grandma Sandy asked, a glint of mischief in her eyes as she helped Grandpa Will to the table.

"No," Rayna answered a bit too quickly. "We were just discussing the evacuation and cattle drive."

"I see." Grandma Sandy's smirk said she didn't believe a word.

"The level three order has been issued."

Grandma Sandy swayed and placed a hand over her heart.

Rayna went to her side. "Are you all right?"

"What if we lose the ranch?" Her grandmother's voice trembled.

Rayna drew her grandmother close. "Worst case, you have insurance."

"It won't cover everything."

"We're going to be all right."

Rayna hoped her words weren't just empty platitudes. While her grandparents did have insurance on the house and outbuildings, they hadn't updated the policy in years. The replacement costs were most certainly insufficient. Worse, they had no insurance on the cattle. They did. Before. But when they sold the last herd, Grandpa Will had canceled the insurance. He hadn't purchased a new policy after he went out and acquired this newest herd, and Grandma Sandy hadn't thought about insurance.

Rayna didn't remind her of the oversight. No good would be served by causing her more distress.

Instead, she changed the subject. "You packed your important papers and jewelry and pictures, right?"

"Yes." Her grandmother didn't sound reassured. "This has been your grandfather's home his entire life and mine since we married sixty years ago."

"I know." Pain squeezed Rayna's heart. She'd always considered the ranch her home away from home. "We have to have faith the fire won't come this way. What is it Pastor Leonard always says? Faith and fear can't exist in the same space."

"What about the people on the north end of the valley? Many of them are friends we've known our entire lives."

Rayna's glance cut to Aden. "The local authorities and firefighters are doing everything they can. Aden's heading there soon to help."

He nodded in response.

"I'm worried about your grandpa," Grandma Sandy whispered, appearing steadier now that the news had sunk in. "He's really confused this morning. This evacuation has upset him."

Rayna turned her attention to her grandfather. He sat staring into his lap and wearing a lost expression. "We'll just have to keep reassuring him."

"It's going to be hard, driving the truck with him in that state," Grandma Sandy said.

"Colton can help keep Grandpa occupied." Even as she said it, she wondered if she was right.

"I'm not sure I can do it all. Herd the cattle, watch your grandpa and Colton."

Rayna felt Aden's eyes on her, questioning.

Her concerns from earlier returned. It was one thing to place demands on herself. Was she being fair placing those same demands on her elderly grandmother? Aden was right, losing the cattle would be devastating, but it was better than losing their lives.

"If you'd rather cut the cattle and other animals loose, we can, Grandma. Then, when we return home, we'll round up as many as we can find."

"If we have a ranch left to bring them to." Grandma Sandy straightened. "No, it's best we drive them. Your grandpa and I need the money."

"If you're sure."

"I am."

"We can stop at any time if you're overwhelmed. There's no shame in that."

Grandma Sandy extracted herself from beneath Rayna's arm as if to demonstrate herself capable of standing on her own two feet. "Let me fix a quick breakfast for everyone, then we can leave." She started toward the pantry. "I hope oatmeal and toast are okay."

Rayna looked again at Aden, seeking his approval for offering to forgo the cattle drive. But whatever opinion he had, he kept it to himself.

"Hurry, Colton." Rayna waved to her son. "He crawled in behind the grain barrels."

They'd managed to capture Nala already. She was the more friendly of the two barn cats and came easily when lured by a plate of wet food. Simba continued to elude them. Suspecting something was up, he'd sprinted away. Rayna and Colton had spent fifteen frustrating minutes chasing him before cornering him at last.

Zip had been no help. The saying about cats being

impossible to herd was true. Simba had outrun and out-smarted the dog until Zip eventually gave up and trotted off to find his new favorite person: Aden.

"Don't let him escape," Rayna shouted at Colton.

She positioned herself on one side of the two barrels and Colton on the other. Blindly reaching in a hand, she grabbed Simba by the neck scruff. While normally sweet-tempered, he hissed and spit and clawed her hand, proving he wasn't a gracious loser.

"Got him!" Rayna straightened and clutched the yowling and squirming cat to her middle.

"Good job, Mommy." Colton sprang to his feet.

"Run and get the carrier."

He did as she asked, returning a minute later half carrying and half dragging the carrier containing Nala. It bounced heavily against his knees with each step, giving the unhappy feline a bumpy ride.

"Okay, good. Put it down and open the door," she told Colton. "Careful, only a little. Don't let Nala out."

Kneeling beside the carrier, Rayna stuffed a very distressed and uncooperative Simba into the carrier, where he curled in the back next to his sister and voiced his displeasure. Loudly.

Her grandparents had acquired the pair of tabbies several years ago from a neighbor when a feral cat delivered her litter beneath their garden shed. Unlike the mother, Nala and Simba had been raised around humans. They even had house privileges when the weather turned cold. That hadn't stopped Simba from being difficult to capture.

"You're bleeding, Mommy," Colton observed when she latched the carrier.

Rayna inspected her hand. "It's not too bad." A few

scratches were the least of her problems. She'd wash it later and apply some ointment. "Let's get these two loaded."

"I'll carry them."

As if being trapped and stuffed into a tiny box wasn't bad enough, the cats had to endure another bumpy walk to the truck. It was nothing compared to what waited ahead—a full day of confinement stuck in a moving vehicle. Rayna hoped the cats settled down at some point and didn't cry the entire time.

Aden and Grandpa Will had hitched the horse trailer to the truck, and the rear door hung open. All three horses were tied to the sides, but only Bisbee was saddled. Fourteen chickens had been gathered and placed in three large dog crates that, along with a sack of chicken feed, had been loaded into the trailer and secured with bungee cords. They sat alongside two five-gallon tanks of fresh water for drinking and washing and just in case the truck overheated.

"Where's Grandpa?" Rayna asked her grandmother when the older woman appeared.

They were getting a later start than anticipated, and the sun had already risen, though it still remained behind the as-yet-untouched eastern mountains. A murky gray blanket covered the sky, giving the illusion of a storm when not a drop of rain was predicted in the forecast.

"He and Aden are fetching the goats," Grandma said.

As if in response, the two men appeared from the direction of the pens, leading the three goats by ropes around their necks. Zip circled behind. A slave to his instincts, he attempted to keep the goats in a tight-knit group. Aden's charge shared the same feelings about being removed from his surroundings as Simba and resisted, digging his dainty hooves into the ground. At his wit's end, Aden stopped and picked up the goat. Holding him tightly to his chest, he carried the bleating goat the remainder of the way where he joined his buddies in the trailer.

"Is that enough hay?" Aden asked Rayna when they were done.

She studied the twelve bales. "It'll have to be. That's all the room we have."

"You doing okay?"

"Yeah. No. I'll feel better once we're on the way." She rubbed her forehead, the enormity of her task sinking in. And always in the forefront of her mind was worry about the ranch and the town. Their friends and neighbors and church family. "Have you heard? Have most people evacuated?"

"Most. Harlan's not the only one staying."

"Seriously! What are they thinking?"

"People are afraid. For some, that makes them want to run away from danger. Others, to stay." Aden removed his cowboy hat and wiped his damp brow.

"Will they be all right? Are the authorities going to intervene?"

"They'll do what they can." He looked down at her bloody hand. "What happened?"

"One of the cats put up a fight."

He took her hand in his and examined the scratches. "You need to be more careful."

His eyes brimming with concern and the warmth of his strong, capable fingers had an instant calming effect on her. He made her think she could do this.

"I wish you were going with us," she blurted and then snapped her mouth shut. "Sorry. I know you can't."

"I wish I could." His gaze roamed her face. "Call me every chance you get."

"I will." She didn't withdraw her hand, and he didn't let go. "Thank you isn't sufficient. You came through for my family. For me. I know it's your job to—"

"I didn't do it because of my job. I think we both know that." A small smile played at the corners of his mouth. "Not entirely."

"When this is over, we're having that talk."

"Rayna."

"I realize a relationship won't be easy. For either of us."

He finally released her. "Are you honestly ready for a man to take Steven's place?"

"I'm still grappling with that part and how I feel," she admitted.

"You wouldn't be human if you weren't." His smile lost some of its charm. "People are going to wonder what you're doing with the likes of me."

"About that." She leveled a finger at him. "One of us needs to work on a change of attitude when this is over."

"If your grandparents weren't right over there, I'd wrap my arms around you."

The fire threatened. The cattle waited in the pasture for the drive to start. Her family needed to get to safety. And yet Rayna allowed herself to sigh with contentment.

"If they weren't right over there, I'd *let* you wrap your arms around me."

The moment was broken when Grandma Sandy hollered, "No, Will. Put them back."

Rayna and Aden both turned to see Grandpa Will struggling to remove a dog crate containing chickens from the trailer's side door.

"What's gotten into you?" he demanded and attempted to shake loose her grip on his arm. "The chickens belong in the coop."

"Will, honey, please." Grandma's Sandy's voice had become strained. "We're evacuating."

"We're doing no such thing!"

"The fire. It's headed toward town."

"What fire?" he roared.

"Can you see it? Right over there. Open your eyes, old man."

He did, staring at the blaze in the distance. "That's near Harlan's place. He must be in trouble."

Rayna sent Aden a concerned look. "Grandpa was okay a minute ago, wasn't he?"

"He seemed perfectly fine to me."

"He's like that sometimes. Switches from coherent to incoherent in a flash. It's getting worse."

"The stress can't be helping."

"I'd better see if Grandma needs me."

Aden waylaid her. "Any chance of him taking off again?"

"Grandma has the truck keys in her pocket, and she hid the spare set. We're not taking any chances."

"Good."

"Hey, Ranger Whitley." Colton and Zip came running over. "Whatcha doing?"

"Glad you're here." He grinned. "I have some important deputy forest ranger instructions to go over with you. Come on."

He winked at Rayna as he took Colton's hand. She

understood—he was freeing her up so she could concentrate on her grandparents. She felt a rush of emotion too early to define.

Grandpa Will seemed particularly confused and uncooperative. As she and Grandma Sandy were trying to reason with him using techniques suggested in the books on dementia they'd read, Claire Weatherby arrived in her truck and trailer. She smiled brightly and signaled, having no clue of the drama ensuing with Grandpa Will. She parked near the Deweys' truck and emerged, taking in her surroundings as she did.

"Morning," she called out. "You've been busy. All ready, I see."

Grandpa Will abruptly stiffened. "What's she doing here?" he demanded.

"She's going to help us drive the cattle, Grandpa," Rayna answered.

"Drive them where?"

Grandma Sandy groaned, losing her patience and forgetting to employ the recommended techniques. "Will, we told you three times already. The fire is headed this way. We're driving the cattle to Tumble Rock."

"Morning, Claire." Rayna left her grandparents and met up with Claire, attempting to deflect trouble. They shook hands. "Thank you again for agreeing to come with us. I can't tell you how much we appreciate it."

"Are you kidding? This is the most excitement I've had in years."

"You're a godsend. We really need you. Is your place secure? Are you okay leaving it?"

"My son drove over from Payson yesterday and got me situated. I'm going to be staying with him and his wife if necessary."

"Let's hope it's not."

"I figured there's nothing I can do about the fire, might as well put myself to good use. If I went to stay with them now, I'd just sit around worrying myself into a frenzy."

Rayna gave the other woman's arm an affectionate squeeze. She stood nearly as tall as Rayna and was almost as trim. She'd worked all her life outdoors, and it showed in a tanned face sculpted by the elements. Her palms bore callouses from years of hard physical labor. Despite being in her early sixties, Claire possessed the strength and stamina to endure the arduous trip. In fact, she'd probably outlast Rayna.

"Howdy, Sandy. Will." Claire lifted her hand to Rayna's grandparents in greeting. "How are you this morning?"

"Well as can be under the circumstances." Grandma Sandy's terse response had nothing to do with Claire and everything to do with Grandpa Will. "And yourself?"

"Same. Trying to remain positive."

Grandpa Will grumbled and stormed off toward the barn. Grandma Sandy started after him only to stop. Expelling a frustrated groan, she pushed a loose strand of pure white hair back from her face before letting her arm drop.

"Grandpa's having a rough morning," Rayna explained to Claire.

"We all are. No one should have to live through a wildfire." Claire unloaded her horse from the trailer. She and Rayna tied the sturdy mare alongside Bisbee. When they'd finished, Claire's glance cut to where Aden was showing Colton how to affix the nozzle on the spare gas tank. "Is he coming with us?"

Rayna tried to detect any rancor in the other woman's tone and found none. Perhaps she wasn't one of those who thought ill of Aden. Rayna hadn't ever spoken to Claire about him. "No. He's returning to work once we're on the way."

"I see," Claire answered with the same neutral tone. She didn't ask for further explanation, and Rayna didn't offer any.

"I could use a hand with the ice chests," Grandma Sandy said.

"I'll help," Claire offered.

The two women went inside, Colton trailing along.

While they were gone, Rayna and Aden made a final inspection of the truck and trailer. She was going through the toolbox when his phone rang.

His features darkened when he glanced at the display. "This is my supervisor."

Rayna watched him in silence while he talked, tension mounting as she listened to his end of the conversation. When he hung up, he relayed what she'd already surmised.

"The fire's reached the northwest edge of the valley. Less than a mile from the firebreak outside town."

"It'll be at the cabin soon! Poor Grandma and Grandpa."

"We'd better get moving."

"I have to grab the wire cutters from the tool room first." She couldn't believe she'd almost forgotten them after what happened the other day on the mountain with the heifer and calf. "Be right back. Can you keep an eye on Grandpa?"

"Sure. Will, you want to help me with the hay?"

They'd loaded the dozen bales in the back of the horse trailer to entice the cattle. Once the hungry cows began walking, the others would follow. Rayna on Bisbee, along with Zip, would bring up the rear. Aden would assist in his truck until they were underway, shutting the gates behind them.

"I don't need a babysitter," Grandpa Will grumbled, nosing around the bed of Claire's truck.

What was with that?

Rayna and Aden exchanged glances before she sped off to the barn, where she quickly located the cutters.

She exited the barn at the same moment her grandmother, Claire and Colton were walking across the yard from the house, each of them carrying a load. Aden stepped out from the horse trailer, brushing the hay off his pants.

The sound of an engine starting gave Rayna a start. It made no sense. Grandma Sandy had the truck keys in her pocket. Rayna increased her pace. Was that… Claire's truck? It couldn't be.

With a clatter that sent a shock wave through Rayna, Claire's truck and trailer backed up and then shot forward, Grandpa Will at the wheel.

Rayna started running. Aden, too.

Grandma Sandy dropped her ice chest and cried, "No! Come back."

Grandpa Will didn't stop and headed down the long drive for the road, the back end of the horse trailer swerving.

Chapter Eight

Rayna blamed herself. Why hadn't she taken her grandfather with her into the barn?

"I'm sorry," Claire said, her voice cracking. "I have one of those keyless ignitions. I keep the fob in my purse, which I left in the truck. I didn't realize it would be a problem."

Rayna didn't respond. Her mind spun a hundred miles an hour. "He must have gone to Harlan's again."

"The old fool." Grandma Sandy burst into tears.

Rayna wanted to comfort her grandmother, but there wasn't time. They had to go after Grandpa. Now. Unlike yesterday, the fire was considerably closer. A mile away from Harlan's. The same wind that whipped their hair and clothes pushed the fire ever closer, foot by foot, second by second. It could reach Harlan's within two hours. Maybe less. He and Grandpa were in serious, life-threatening danger.

She turned to Aden as naturally as if he'd always been there for her and always would be. "What do we do?"

He held up a hand to silence her. It was then she realized he was already on the phone with the sheriff's department, reporting Grandpa missing, giving a description of the vehicle and his likely destination. The thirty-second pause while he listened to their response felt like an eternity. Rayna balled her hands into tight fists so hard her nails dug into her palms.

They'd gathered outside and stood behind the house in a small cluster. Grandma continued to bemoan how she knew better than to have let Grandpa wander off unsupervised. Claire kept apologizing for something she couldn't possibly have prevented and wasn't the least bit responsible for. Colton tugged on Rayna's shirttail, asking one question after another. She willed the three of them to be quiet so that she could concentrate on Aden's call with the sheriff's department. At last, he hung up and turned to face her.

"Well?"

"They'll try to send someone out there."

"Try?" She couldn't believe she'd heard correctly.

"Rayna, they're busy. The fire has reached several vacation homes in the lower mountains north of Happenstance and the Elk Ridge Lodge. It's chaos out there."

"It's chaos here."

"They'll do everything they possibly can." He started toward his truck without looking back.

She chased after him. "Where are you going?"

"To Harlan's."

"I'm coming with you. Grandma, watch Colton for me," she shouted the last part over her shoulder.

"No." Aden ground to a halt and whirled on her. "You stay here."

"No way." She muscled past him.

He caught her by the arm and swung her around. "I'm not joking, Rayna."

"And neither am I." She squared her shoulders and glared up at him. "You need me. Grandpa won't be co-operative."

"I have training. I'm used to removing people from dangerous situations."

"Not people with dementia."

His resistance lasted only a moment longer before his expression softened. She felt his touch before he captured her hand in his. "I couldn't bear it if anything happened to you."

"I couldn't bear it if something happened to Grandpa and I could have stopped it."

"You are the stubbornest person I know."

"I am. Especially when I care about something. Or someone," she added, letting him know she wasn't just referring to her grandfather.

He must have understood for he squeezed her fingers. What he didn't do was agree to take her along.

"I'm just going to follow you in the ranch pickup," she said. "You might as well say yes."

He grumbled under his breath. "Promise you'll listen and follow my directions. Otherwise, I'm tossing you out. I don't care where we are."

He was lying, of course. He wouldn't toss her out.

"I promise."

"Swear?"

"Aden."

A helicopter appeared from the south and flew overhead, lower to the ground than the ones the previous day. Like before, a bucket filled with water dangled from its belly and appeared close enough to touch. For a moment, Rayna and Aden ceased talking, unable to hear above the deafening sound. She looked for Colton, who stood not far away, staring up at the helicopter in amazement and excitement. He didn't quite grasp the situation or the peril they were in. Beside him, Zip barked furiously.

On impulse, Rayna ran over to her son as the helicopter passed them on its path toward the fire. She bent down and pulled him into a brief but fierce hug.

"I love you more than anything in the world. Be good for Grandma, okay? I'll be back soon."

"Why can't I go with you?"

"Because it's your job to watch over Grandma and the ranch." That was all she could manage. The lump in her throat prevented her from continuing.

Tearing herself away from him required all her willpower. Next, she hugged her grandmother.

"If we're not back in an hour, you get Colton out of here. Understand? Cut the cattle loose and free the animals. Don't worry about them." Maybe Aden had been right all along.

"Rayna, we're not leaving without you."

"Yes, you are. Grandma, I've never been more serious in my life. Whatever happens, save Colton."

"God will bring you and your grandfather home safe. Aden, too. I'm convinced."

"Me, too."

At least, Rayna longed to be sure. She'd been sure Steven would return home that day he'd stopped at the gas station, and then he hadn't. If she could have prevented his death, she'd have gladly taken any risk.

"I'll make sure Sandy and your son leave in an hour," Claire said. "You have my word."

"Thank you."

Blinking back tears, Rayna ran after Aden, who was already climbing into the truck. As they pulled out, she waved to her son, grandmother and Claire, telling herself she would see them again when they brought Grandpa Will home. She pictured this exact same scene only in reverse—her and Aden pulling into the drive with Grandpa and Harlan sitting in the back and the family greeting them with smiles on their faces.

Once underway, she stared ahead in amazement, shocked at the progress the fire had made overnight. The huge layer of smoke, now twice its previous size, curled in on itself like a giant wave. The flames were so huge she could discern tiny details, like how the colors changed hue as the fire expanded and contracted.

What surprised her the most was the noise when Aden rolled down the window and motioned an oncoming vehicle to give them room to safely pass. Like a freight train coming straight for them.

Hot perspiration turned into a cold sweat. In contrast, Aden appeared unaffected by the alarming sights and commotion and just kept driving, purpose etched in his features.

In the distance, a siren blared and grew ominously closer.

"What's that?" she asked, peering ahead and then looking behind them.

"Emergency vehicles. Either coming or going."

As if in answer, an ambulance materialized ahead, a dim outline at first and then becoming clearer as it neared.

"Has someone been hurt?" she asked.

It was, Rayna realized, a rhetorical question. Yes,

someone had been hurt. The ambulance was traveling away from the fire, not toward it. Likely they were taking the east road to the hospital in Globe. Could they get through? According to the last radio report, traffic on the road was bumper to bumper.

"I hope they'll be all right," she said as Aden slowed the truck and pulled over to the side to let the ambulance pass.

He clenched his jaw, the muscles visibly working. There was no small talk today. All his attention was focused on the road and getting to Harlan's.

They drove for another ten minutes, this time in silence. One more bend in the road, another half mile, and then they'd reach the road to Harlan's. Rayna's knee bobbed in nervous anticipation. Before long, this would all be over. She didn't care what they had to do, what lengths they had to go to, they'd save Grandpa and Harlan.

They flew around the bend, the rear tires fishtailing in the dirt road's loose gravel. Rayna gasped and grabbed the dash with both hands when the front passenger's side wheels dropped off at the edge of the road, and the truck tilted.

"Please," she whispered. "Don't let us roll."

Aden hollered, "Hold on," and muscled the steering wheel.

Through sheer determination, he righted the truck, showing admirable skill. When they were once again speeding along, she let out her breath and pried loose her hands from the dash, only to discover they were shaking uncontrollably.

"Are you okay?" Aden asked with incredible calm.

"That was kind of close," she admitted, her voice weak. "I'll try to be more careful next time."

"Next time?"

And then, as if to defy his words, he slammed on the brakes, sending the truck skidding. They zigzagged momentarily before coming to a gut-twisting stop. The seat belt harness cut into Rayna's right shoulder and triggered a sharp pain.

She yelped as the force thrust her backward into the seat. "What's going on?"

"We can't get through."

"We can't get through?" she repeated dumbly. "How can... I don't understand."

She stared ahead, her mind slowly absorbing the pair of official SUVs blocking the road not thirty feet ahead. They were parked front end to front end and formed an impassable barrier. A sandwich board sign sat on the ground in front of them with a bright red Stop and Road Closed printed in big letters. Two deputy sheriffs, each of them sporting a white cowboy hat and aviator sunglasses, stood together beside the sign. They both glanced up and the taller one motioned for Rayna and Aden to turn around, hollering something she couldn't understand.

"They must have just closed the road," Aden said. "I didn't get the call yet."

"But that's the way to Harlan's. What about Grandpa?"

"He had to have driven by before the deputies arrived."

None of this made any sense to her. "We have to get to Harlan's." She grabbed Aden's arm, her panic escalating to a level she hadn't felt since Steven's death. "We can't let Grandpa or Harlan die in the fire."

"Sit tight." He opened the truck door and jumped out.

Rayna ignored the order and stumbled out after him. Aden made straight for the two deputy sheriffs, ignoring Rayna, who followed behind, half running to keep up.

"I'm Ranger Aden Whitley with the US Forest Service." He withdrew his ID and showed the two uniformed men. "We're searching for a missing person. William Dewey. He's a resident of Happenstance and in his early eighties. He was last seen driving a red Chevy pickup and pulling an empty white two-horse trailer. He likely came this way five, maybe ten minutes ago. Have you seen him?"

"No one in a red Chevy pickup." The taller deputy swapped looks with his partner, mild annoyance showing on their faces. "We just got here ourselves a few minutes ago."

"Can you let us pass?" Aden asked, respectful but firm. "We believe he's gone to Harlan Gilligan's place off the 243."

"No can do, buddy. This road's closed," the shorter deputy answered.

By then, another vehicle had arrived and stopped behind Aden's truck. The shorter deputy raised his arm and motioned to the driver for him to turn around and head back. When the man hesitated, he repeated the motion with more emphasis. All the while, Rayna's anxiety escalated until she thought she might kick the nearest tire in frustration. Lives were at risk. Were the deputies being intentionally obtuse?

Finally the vehicle behind them turned around and left. Fed up, Rayna tried to push past Aden, intending to confront the deputies, but he held her back with an arm made of iron.

She didn't care and blurted, "You've got to help us. My grandfather has dementia. He doesn't fully grasp what's happening and is unaware of the danger he's in. Don't you make exceptions for people who are impaired?"

The shorter deputy's stony features gentled. "I'm really sorry about your grandfather, ma'am. But we can't let you by. We're under orders. We could lose our jobs. Which is no big deal compared to the two of you losing your lives."

"But my grandfather!" Rayna wanted to weep almost as much as she wanted to scream.

"Look. Can you at least do us a favor?" Aden asked. "Advise headquarters? There are two old men up there who can't possibly get out on their own if, when, the fire makes it that way. I'm sure your office is familiar with Harlan Gilligan. They've sent deputies to his place plenty of times."

"I know Harlan," the taller deputy admitted. He hesitated for several seconds before relenting. "All right. I'll call as soon as you two hightail it out of here. You have my word, Ranger Whitley."

"Thanks. Appreciate it."

"Could you —"

Aden cut Rayna off. "Let's go. There's nothing more to be done here."

"But we need to get to Harlan's place."

"I know a detour."

They ran back to his truck and climbed in. Aden threw the truck into Reverse and barreled down the road the way they'd come. "Better grab on to something. This is going to be one rough ride."

They covered the next half mile slowly while Aden searched to his left for the long-ago-abandoned road.

He recalled overgrown foliage hid the entrance. Smoke and flying ash made it more difficult to spot.

He'd traveled the abandoned road only a handful of times. One of those was to rescue a coworker who'd been chased up a tree by a pack of wild dogs. They'd wandered the area for months, causing trouble for campers and hikers before they were finally caught. The pack had surprised Aden's coworker during a routine tree-marking expedition. Or maybe he'd surprised the dogs. Either way, he'd sat with legs dangling from an upper branch for several hours until reinforcements arrived.

"Should we call Search and Rescue?" Rayna asked, a tremor in her voice. One minute, she appeared ready to charge into the fire single-handed to save her grandfather. The next, she hovered on the verge of a breakdown.

"They'd send the closest person, and that's me."

He sensed she wanted to say more, insist there was someone else they could contact. Instead, she balled her hands in her lap and, he was pretty sure, gritted her teeth.

Aden wished there was more he could do. "Let me try the ranger station." Picking up the radio with one hand while keeping the other on the steering wheel, he pressed the button. "Garver District Ranger Station, this is Ranger Aden Whitley. Over."

"Come in, Ranger Whitley."

He recognized the voice. "Martin, I'm with Rayna Karstetter. Her grandfather, Will Dewey, has gone missing. We're heading to Harlan Gilligan's now. We figure he's there. Just in case he isn't, can you alert the other rangers on duty? Ask them to radio in if they've seen Will and pass the info to me? He's driving a red

Chevy pickup and pulling an empty white two-horse trailer. Over."

"Affirmative, Aden. Can do. Over."

"Appreciate that, pal. Over and out."

"Thank you," Rayna said, sending him an appreciative smile.

"Don't know how much help it'll be."

"Better than nothing."

Before he could reassure her they would find her grandfather, he broke into a racking cough and buried his face in the crook of his left arm.

"Are you all right?" Rayna asked.

He brought his cough under control and croaked, "Yeah."

"You don't sound all right."

"I'll be fine."

In truth, his lungs burned and his throat felt raw. He'd forgotten his bandanna in their rush to leave, not that it provided much protection. Even inside the truck there was no escaping the smoke's acrid odor and foul taste, which poured in through the air-conditioning vents.

Were he honest with himself, smoke wasn't the only reason his lungs were giving him grief. He'd been breathing heavily for over thirty minutes now, a combination of adrenaline and nerves. If he didn't give himself a rest soon, or find some fresh air, he'd suffer one of those unpleasant side effects the doctor had warned him about.

Except there was no resting now. Not until they found Will.

"There it is," he nearly shouted when the entrance to the old road materialized.

Braking abruptly, he executed a sharp left, and they

breached the overgrown entrance. The immediate steep incline resembled the first giant climb on a roller coaster ride. The truck's wheels groaned and complained as they crawled over boulders, sunk in and then climbed out of holes, and avoided decades-old, rotted logs.

"This truck has four-wheel drive, doesn't it?" Rayna sputtered as she was repeatedly knocked side to side.

"Standard equipment for a forest ranger vehicle."

She lowered her head and peered out the windshield. "I feel like we're in a tunnel. The kind from a nightmare."

Her description wasn't far off. The truck's headlights were useless against the thick foliage and darkened sky. They had no idea how far they'd come or how far ahead the main road lay. Aden leaned forward, fighting the pull of gravity that insisted on sucking him into the seat back. Rayna, too.

"Where did this road even come from?" she asked loud enough to be heard over the cacophony of noise from spinning tires, tree limbs attacking the truck and the engine protesting every obstacle they encountered. "I had no idea it existed."

"The miners originally used it to transport supplies."

"By horseback?"

"Mostly. And mules." They bounced over a particularly deep hole. Items in the console popped out of their compartments and fell onto the floor. "Leave it," Aden said when Rayna attempted to reach for a pack of gum that had landed at her feet. "Don't hurt yourself." When they were on a slightly less rugged patch of road, he continued. "The road was better maintained in those days. After the silver played out around World War I, the miners left the area, and the road went to ruin."

"No kidding." Rayna's head bumped into the window. "Ouch!"

"You okay?"

"I'll live." She rubbed the spot. "Ever rescue anyone stuck here?"

"More than once."

A few daring hunters and hikers occasionally went head-to-head with the road, determined to test their mettle. Some made it to the top. Most turned back. One had to be towed when the oil pan cracked while going over a large boulder and drained the engine of oil. Aden had been part of the search and rescue team that located a honeymooning couple lost last winter when they'd wandered off the road in search of a photo op.

"How much longer?" Rayna asked a moment later. "I think all my insides have shifted. My stomach's where my kidneys are supposed to be."

"I'm not sure."

Aden concentrated, his right temple pounding. Possibly another side effect of physical exertion on top of his smoke inhalation. What had made him think the doctor would medically clear him today?

And then it happened. Weak sunlight filtered in from above where seconds earlier there'd been none. A small opening loomed ahead, beckoning them. Aden pushed the truck for everything it was worth, as if their very lives depended on reaching the main road. Maybe Will's and Harlan's did. A dozen last slaps from branches and scrapes from bushes, and they were free of the nightmare tunnel. The truck bucked twice as it landed on the flat ground.

"Thank God," Rayna exclaimed and clasped Aden's arm. "You were amazing."

"We're not there yet." He took a moment to gain his bearings and then turned right, flooring the gas pedal. Five more minutes to Harlan's.

"Any ideas how we'll get Grandpa to come with us if he refuses? He won't want to leave Harlan behind."

"I don't know."

"I guess we try talking some sense into them." She chewed her lower lip. "Think you can overpower them?"

"Let's just get there and then decide. See whether or not Will is confused. He and Harlan may come willingly. If not, I won't risk injuring them, or us, by engaging in a struggle."

"No. Of course not. I just thought they might have taught you a technique in Search and Rescue."

"Mostly to reason with the person and keep reasoning."

"Which is impossible if Grandpa is in one of his states." She resumed chewing her lower lip.

Aden slowed as a trio of deer sprinted across the road well ahead of them—two does and a fawn still with its white spots. He'd have thought the deer smart enough to have fled long before now. The fire was a mile away last he'd heard. Perhaps they'd gotten separated from their herd. Smoke and fire could interfere with an animal's instincts, confusing them.

"What if we tell him that Grandma's sick and needs him?" Rayna asked. "I'm not opposed to lying under these circumstances."

"That might work."

"I'll say she's having chest pains and thinks it's a heart attack."

"Just be convincing."

"What about Harlan?" Rayna's expression spoke volumes. "We can't leave him, and Grandma's fake chest pains won't sway him."

"I don't know, Rayna. One problem at time."

Her cell phone rang before she could say more. As Aden suspected, the call was from home, Sandy checking to see if they'd found Will yet.

"No, Grandma. We had to take a detour. The sheriff's department closed the road."

Aden could hear Sandy's raised voice through Rayna's phone. She did her best to reassure her frantic grandmother but had little success.

"I'll call you as soon as we know something. How's Colton?...Okay, that's good. The fire's still five miles from the ranch...No, I don't care. You leave...I'm absolutely serious. I can't be looking for Grandpa and fretting about you and Colton. Promise me, Grandma... Yes. Will do...Love you, too."

She disconnected, her dire expression reflecting her conflicting emotions. He didn't have any children, but he could imagine how difficult it was for her leaving Colton in someone else's care during a time like this.

A siren broke the silence. They pulled far to the side to let the fire engine pass. Aden noticed Rayna nervously eyeing the drop-off, probably remembering their close call earlier. She breathed an audible sigh of relief when Aden pulled ahead and away from the edge.

She had more courage than most people he knew. Certainly more grit and determination. Heights, however, must be her Achilles' heel.

The drive leading to Harlan's house at long last came into view. Aden swung onto it and pushed the engine yet again to make the grueling climb in record time. The last few days had taken a toll on his poor truck.

He didn't care. All that mattered was finding Will and ensuring all the Deweys reached safety.

As they neared, the roof of Harlan's house appeared. Then the house itself. Next, the shed and outbuilding.

And that was all!

The driveway was empty as was the covered parking area next to the shed, apart from Harlan's ATV. No one came out from behind the house. Curtains covered the widows, and the shed door, normally secured with a large padlock, hung open.

It was the worst kind of déjà vu imaginable. Once again, they'd guessed wrong about Will's whereabouts.

"He's not here!" Rayna cried, heaving herself out of the truck.

Aden chased after her. "He probably went to the cabin for his brother's chest."

She stopped and spun to stare at him with wide eyes. "You're right! Why didn't we realize that from the start? Let's hurry!"

"We should search for Harlan first. He may be hiding somewhere he believes will keep him safe from the fire. I'll look." Aden pointed to the truck. "You lay on the horn. See if that brings him out."

Rayna did. She must have been putting the entirety of her frustration and anxiety into the task for the piercing sound echoed through the surrounding woods. It roused no one. Aden made a running two-minute check of the premises, determining that Harlan had most likely left.

"Can you call the sheriff's department to find out for sure?" Rayna asked.

"They're busy with the evacuation. I doubt they have the resources." An idea occurred to Aden. "It's possible he left with your grandfather and the two of them are heading back to the ranch."

"Do you think?" Hope sprang in Rayna's eyes.

"Call your grandmother. Tell her what we suspect. In the meantime, we'll head to the cabin just in case we're wrong."

Rayna started for the truck. She got only a few steps before bursting into sobs.

Aden didn't think. He went to her and pulled her into his arms, cradling the back of her head with his palm as she buried her face in his shirt.

"Shh, Rayna, don't cry."

"I know. It's not helping. We need to get on the road. Just give me a minute."

He kissed the top of her curls, which had become a wild mess during their ride up the old mining road. As he did, his chest swelled, filling with an emotion Aden hadn't felt for a woman before.

In that instant, he knew he would lay down his life for Rayna and do whatever was humanly possible to find and save her grandfather. He'd also walk through fire if necessary to be with her—now and forever.

She may not feel the same for him. That was something they could explore later when this terrible ordeal was over. For now, he had a mission. He knew it with absolute certainty, as if God had spoken directly to him.

"I'm going to drop you off at the ranch."

"No!" She drew back to stare at him. "That's out of the way. What if Grandpa didn't go there and went after his brother's chest?"

"The fire's too close to the cabin. Closer than here. Definitely closer than the ranch. I won't risk your life." He'd never forgive himself if she was injured…or worse.

"Please, Aden. Take me with you. You may need my help with Grandpa."

"I'll manage."

Tears streamed down her cheeks. "I can't stay behind only to lose another loved one."

"Rayna, honey, it's too dangerous. I have training. You don't."

She wiped angrily at her face. Or was that determinedly? "I wasn't there when Steven died. I might have been able to save him if I had been."

"There was nothing you could have done."

"We don't know that." Her voice rose. "But I do know I can help save Grandpa."

"You want Colton to lose both his parents?"

"I trust you, Aden." She met his gaze, and hers didn't waver. "You won't let that happen to me."

"I won't," he said with a confidence he hadn't felt until that very second. "Come on. We need to hurry."

They jumped back into the truck with renewed purpose. Failing wasn't an option.

Chapter Nine

As soon as Aden and Rayna were in the truck and moving again, he radioed Garver District Ranger Station. With luck, they'd provide him with the latest update on the fire. He also intended to ask about Will and Harlan. The same dispatcher Aden had spoken to on the way to Harlan's place responded to his hail.

"Come in, Ranger Whitley. Have you located William Dewey?"

"Not yet. He wasn't at Harlan Gilligan's. The place is abandoned. We're hoping he's on his way back to the Dewey ranch along with Harlan. He may also be at the family cabin just north of Aspen Lane Crossing and lumber road number 137. Are you able to give us an estimate on the distance of the fire from there? Over."

"Hold on a minute."

Aden set the radio unit down on the console. He felt Rayna's tension from across the short distance separating them. It sucked every molecule of air from the truck cab.

He tried but couldn't fathom the weight of her fears. Aden's own troubles paled in comparison. What did it matter that some people thought poorly of him? Or that his family refused to have anything to do with him? Both things were beyond his control—and his caring at the moment.

He'd sacrifice all his earthly possessions, do everything within his power, to find Will and make sure Rayna's family remained safe. That *she* remained safe.

God, he'd been a fool to bring her along. He should have dropped her off at the ranch. Or a friend's house. A friend with a vehicle so she could evacuate with them. Her heartfelt reminder of her late husband had weakened his resolve. Please let him not regret his actions.

He sent Rayna a look. Beneath the fear shining in her eyes a spark of courage flashed. She would slay dragons for those she loved—and he would do the same for her.

This was his calling, he knew in that instant. The direction God had intended for him all along. More than being a forest ranger and protecting the environment. More than volunteering for Search and Rescue. All his training, all his experience and education, had led him here to this day. And this woman.

A shift occurred inside his chest. It was, he realized with newfound clarity, a lifetime's worth of anger and resentment crumbling away. Rayna alone had done that for him when nothing and no one had before.

The next instant, his radio came to life, and he grabbed it off the console.

"Aden, are you there? This is Garver District Ranger station. Come in."

"Aden here, Martin. What did you learn? Over."

"Incident Command's last report puts the fire at approximately three-quarters of a mile from that area. Over."

Rayna gasped and turned eyes wide with alarm on Aden.

"When was the last report?" he asked Martin.

"Fifteen minutes ago."

"What's the wind speed?"

"Thirty-two miles per hour and picking up fast."

"Copy that."

Aden's stomach clenched. With the wind at its current speed, it wouldn't be long before the fire reached the cabin. *If* it did. It might veer off in another direction at the last minute or split and miss the cabin entirely. There was simply no telling.

"Thanks, Martin. Over and—"

"Wait," the dispatcher cut in. "Ranger Douglas just entered the station. He reports spotting Harlan Gilligan at the evacuation center in town. Over."

A jolt shot through Aden. "Was William Dewey with him?"

Rayna must have experienced the same jolt for she leaned closer to Aden, her expression intent.

"Hold on." The pause that followed seemed to last an hour rather than a minute. "Ranger Douglas reports no. Harlan was alone. Sorry, Aden."

"Thanks for your help. If there are any changes in the fire, let me know. We're heading to the cabin now. Over."

"Be careful."

"Roger that. Over and out."

Aden's spirits sank. Rayna's, too. She leaned back into her seat, looking crestfallen.

"You should call your grandmother," he said, slowing to take a turn in the road. "Give her an update."

"I'm not sure I have the heart."

"Talk to Colton. He needs his mom right now."

She nodded and picked up her phone. In an artificially carefree voice, she carried on a lively conversation with her son, describing the fire in subdued terms so as not to alarm him and constantly telling him to be a good boy and leave with his great-grandma even if she and Aden weren't back yet. When she finished, she disconnected and stared for several silent minutes out the window, the thump of the windshield wipers clocking the passing moments.

Visibility diminished with each bend they rounded. The smoke—as his dad had been fond of saying—was thick enough to choke a snake. It didn't hide the flames, however. They leaped high from the tops of trees, plundering the woods Aden knew and loved.

A fire truck came up behind them, appearing from nowhere, its horn blaring loud enough to rattle the truck windows. Aden swerved out of the way and came to a stop. The right front tire went into a ditch, leaving the truck at an angle. Rayna gasped and squeezed her eyes shut. The fire truck passed them with only inches to spare. The firefighters hanging off the sides waved at them—not in greeting but motioning for them to turn around. Cranking the steering wheel, Aden straightened the truck and got them back on the road. Rayna relaxed, marginally, and stared at the flickering flames. Bright orange and red, they expanded and shrunk, rose and fell, in a macabre dance. Their edges, softened by the dense smoke, were merely an illusion that fooled no one. These flames had no mercy. They had the ability

to destroy entire mountain ranges and countless lives—
animal and human.

"Aden." Rayna's tremulous voice broke his concentration. "I'm afraid."

"I know, honey. I am, too."

"What if we're too late to save Grandpa?"

"We won't be." He peered in the direction of the
cabin, his jaw clenched. The fire was closing fast. He
reminded himself his eyes could be playing tricks on
him. Distances were impossible to accurately judge in
these conditions. "We'll find him."

Though any distraction was risky, he reached for
Rayna's hand and brought it to his lips for a quick kiss.
When he would have let go, she held on and brought
his hand to her lips. The sweet kiss she planted there
lingered. She met his gaze before letting go, speaking with her heart rather than words. Aden cradled her
cheek briefly and then returned his hand to the wheel.

The moment had a surreal quality about it. Here they
were, racing toward a wildfire, searching for her missing grandfather, courting danger, and yet he'd remember this brief exchange for the rest of his days.

Many, many days. Aden was more determined than
ever to locate Will. Especially now that he had something worth fighting for.

He almost missed the turnoff to the cabin. Hitting
the brakes, he white-knuckled the steering wheel as the
truck's tires skidded on the dirt road. Rayna squealed.
Aden swung the truck right and plowed ahead.

A half mile to go. They didn't talk during the strenuous ascent. Between the dense trees, thick ground cover
and rugged road conditions, Aden needed to concentrate. Though not as rough a ride as the detour to Har-

lan's place, he and Rayna were still jostled about in their seats. She let out a few low grunts and repeatedly braced her palms on the dash, but otherwise remained mute.

He dared a quick look at her, struck by her resolute expression. Brave or stubborn, he wasn't sure which. Once again, he wished he'd left her behind. Once again, he vowed to protect her at all costs.

If they had to abandon the search for Will in order to save Rayna, he would. He didn't care what argument she made, how many tears she cried or how vehemently she protested, he'd get her out of there. He was certain God would understand and forgive him. He was also certain Will would understand and forgive him. The old man loved his granddaughter and wouldn't want her to endanger herself for him.

"Wait! What's that?" Rayna hollered, breaking Aden's concentration.

"Where?"

"Ahead. See that spot of red through those trees to the left."

Aden slowed the truck. A spot of red did indeed appear between the trees. He pulled entirely off the side of the road to avoid being struck by another vehicle. Squinting out the window, he studied the spot.

"Is it Claire's truck?" Rayna asked, her nerves evident in her shaky voice.

"I can't tell from here." They were too far away, and the smoke too thick for him to distinguish the blurry shape. "Why would your grandfather drive into the woods and then park?"

"He has dementia. He's not always in the present but somewhere, sometime, in the past. We have no idea what he might have been thinking."

"Hand me the binoculars."

They'd fallen onto the passenger's side floor during the ride. Rayna bent and retrieved them, passing them to Aden. He peered through the eyepieces and adjusted the focus.

"Is it him?" she asked.

"Looks big enough to be a vehicle, but beyond that I'm not sure." He squinted, trying again to make out details. The next second, he heard the door open and dropped the binoculars. "Rayna, what are you doing?"

"That's the same color red as Claire's truck. It could be Grandpa. I'm going to find out."

He reached for her arm but grabbed only air. She was already out and on the ground, skirting the front of the truck and darting across the road. Groaning under his breath, Aden shut off the engine, shoved his own door open and went after her.

"Rayna," he hollered.

Smoldering ash invaded his nose and mouth. Smoke stung his eyes. His mind returned to when he'd been driving the bulldozer and had suffered smoke inhalation.

Rayna didn't heed his repeated calls or slow down. Ignoring his discomfort as best he could, he pulled his shirt up to cover his mouth and nose. The inadequate barrier provided no help, and he struggled for every breath as he continued after her. Normally, he'd easily outrun her. Not today. The insufferable heat alone would drain a person of all their energy. Add his compromised lungs to that, and he had zero chance of catching up with her.

With each pounding step, Aden's heavy boots crushed the undergrowth beneath them. A lighted ember landed on his pant leg. Another ember landed on his left arm. Without either thinking or slowing, he slapped at them both with his right hand.

"Rayna," he hollered again. He doubted his rough and choked voice carried more than a few feet.

He stumbled once and kept going. By now, his legs threatened to give out, and his side cramped. If this was Claire's truck, please, God, let Will be sitting in it, safe and unharmed. If not, Rayna wouldn't hesitate. She'd head straight into the fire to search for him. If that happened, Aden would do whatever was necessary to stop her. Tackle her. Throw her over his shoulder and carry her out kicking and screaming.

Just as another cough overtook him, she ground to a stop. The reason became instantly clear. A bright red vehicle sat fifty feet in the distance. Nestled against a tree, scrub brush clung to its tires and dead pine needles covered the roof and hood. The driver's side door was missing.

Aden finally caught up with Rayna. Putting an arm on her shoulder, he squeezed. The two of them stared at the abandoned SUV.

"I'm sorry," he said.

Rayna bit back a sob "I was so sure it was him."

"We need to get back. Right now."

He glanced at the fire, chillingly close now. It must be moving faster than predicted, in this area at least. Had the winds increased? Aden couldn't tell. But one thing he knew with dreadful certainty, they had little more than an hour before the fire reached the cabin, if that.

Rayna pivoted and started out at a fast walk, visibly fighting her disappointment. Aden captured her hand in his and began jogging. Exhausted as he was, as difficult as it was to breathe, they couldn't afford to delay.

She kept pace with him, the urgency propelling them both forward. At the truck, Aden stood for just a minute, giving his body a brief rest and gathering his courage for what the next ten minutes were going to bring. He hoped against hope they wouldn't face the same disappointment when they reached the cabin. What would they do if Will wasn't there?

Inside the truck, he again hit the gas and continued their ascent up the steep, narrow and rocky road, ten times more treacherous than on a normal day.

"We're going to find him, Rayna," he said as much for her peace of mind as his own.

She nodded.

They rounded yet another bend. The flames on this side were huge, and Aden's gut clenched. He'd had a similar reaction the other day when he'd been helping the firefighters. Most flames burning the forest floor averaged a meter tall. These were no exception and spread from one spot to the next at remarkable speed. One cluster of flames suddenly jumped to a height of nearly three meters before ebbing, spurred by a gust of oxygen-rich wind. Wildfires had the ability to create their own weather, which only hampered firefighters' efforts.

Aden estimated the flames were no more than the length of a football field away. Here, he reminded himself. The cabin was a quarter mile ahead. The fire may not be as close there.

Then again, it may be destroying the cabin right this second. Please, not with Will inside.

Was there time to radio the ranger station for an update?

"My God!" Rayna exclaimed and pointed out her window.

Aden looked just in time to see a tree engulfed in flames hit the ground not fifty yards away. He'd been wrong in his calculations about the fire's distance. They heard the crash from the tree despite the closed windows. A cloud of charred bark and limbs exploded into the air above the fallen tree as they passed. Rayna continued watching the awful spectacle in the side mirror.

Not Aden. He pressed ahead, relieved they were leaving this area and entering one less treacherous.

Could the fire have diverged and taken a different path? One that passed the cabin. He hoped so, for there was no going back now.

Rayna had only been this scared once before in her life: when Steven had died. That had been a different kind of fear, however. A fear with no edges and no end in sight. How would she be able to continue alone without her beloved husband beside her? Was one income sufficient to ensure her son's health and happiness and meet all his needs? What did the future hold for the two of them? Would she ever wake up in the morning and not be racked with guilt and grief, loneliness and depression?

The fear she felt today curled icy fingers around her insides and squeezed until her blood ran cold. It leaned in close and whispered in her ear that any attempts she and Aden made were futile, they couldn't change the outcome. Her beloved grandfather was doomed. The cattle were lost. Her grandmother would be left a penniless widow. She and Aden had no chance of surviving.

And then she heard the other voice, the one from above, and the icy fingers released their grip. For a while after Steven's death, she hadn't listened to Him. Now, she let God's power and love fill her and bring her comfort.

God had a plan. She believed it with all her being. He'd guided her this far and would see her through. She pressed a hand over her heart and closed her eyes, replaying His words in her head.

The truck suddenly hit a pothole, and Rayna's eyes flew open as she was thrust against the seat belt harness. Looking around, she knew immediately where they were. Aden, too. Recognition sparked in his blue eyes.

Thank you, Lord, for sending him to me. I could never have done this alone.

"The cabin's up ahead," she said even though Aden knew that already.

At a sharp pain in her palms, she glanced down to see her fingernails digging into her flesh. Her grandpa had to be there. *He must be.* She visualized Claire's truck parked in front of the suspension bridge, her grandfather sitting behind the wheel.

"Rayna," Aden said with a voice like steel. "If your grandfather's not there—"

"Don't say it. He will be."

He will, he will, he will.

The truck crested the last rise, the front tires scrambling for traction as they hit level road. Rayna gripped the armrest for support. The windshield wipers *whump-*

whumped as they struggled to clear away the ash and embers sticking to the glass like glue.

A second later they saw it. Claire's red truck and white horse trailer sat parked askew, exactly where Rayna had imagined them. A sob escaped her throat as relief unlike anything she'd experienced before rendered her weak. She clasped her trembling hands together in gratitude.

"He's here!" Not sitting behind the wheel but here somewhere.

"Thank God," Aden said.

Yes. Thank God. And Aden for getting them here safely.

He pulled up behind the horse trailer and parked. Without waiting for her, he shut off the engine and jumped out. Rayna followed suit on wobbly legs barely able to support her.

In the woods above and behind the run-down cabin, a hundred yards away, the fire blazed. Burning embers rained on them like volcanic ash. Rayna swatted at the ones making contact, feeling a quick sting before extinguishing them. The scarf covering her nose and mouth was no more effective than fish netting, and each breath she drew was an effort.

Poor Aden. He must be suffering far worse than she.

A deafening roar came from nowhere, and they both turned. It sounded like a rockslide or an avalanche. No, a hundred bass drums being beaten simultaneously. She had to stop herself from cowering.

"Is that the fire?" she asked.

"Yeah."

She stared in amazement. Dark, angry smoke surged upward from the trees in enormous black and gray plumes. It blocked every speck of sunlight and buried the cabin in an ominous shadow. Rayna refused to consider for even a second that the shadow foretold what she and Aden would find inside. Grandpa Will was fine. All they had to do was cross the bridge, go into the cabin and bring him out. Then drive out of there as fast as possible. They'd have to leave Claire's truck and horse trailer behind. Couldn't be helped. Their lives came first.

She and Aden ran single file to the rickety suspension bridge only to pull up short. How had Grandpa managed to cross? The ancient contraption appeared on the verge of collapse. It swayed side to side in the strong wind, the wooden planks clattering. A loose plank dangled from one end by a frayed rope. That hadn't been there yesterday. The handrails sagged to knee-height. Fortunately, the stakes holding the bridge, their entire lengths driven deep into concrete footings, appeared sound.

Okay. The bridge must be strong enough to cross. Grandpa Will had done it, right? Or had he?

Rayna inched forward and peered over the edge of the ravine to the rocky and scraggly bottom, pure terror coursing through her veins. Her already unsteady legs began to shake violently. Her stomach pitched, and her head swam.

Aden clutched her arm and jerked her back. "Rayna! Be careful."

Slowly, the dizziness passed. "He didn't fall in the ravine," she croaked.

"Is that what you thought?"

"I guess."

"The cabin door is open. Didn't you see?"

She looked. Just as Aden had said, the door stood wide, slightly crooked because of the worn hinges. It had been like that for years, Rayna thought, her mind briefly drifting.

Aden started for the suspension bridge. "I need to hurry. The fire's getting closer." At the foot of the bridge, he stopped and spun.

"You wait here," he instructed. "I'll get your grandfather and be back."

"I'm coming with you."

"No, Rayna. If the fire reaches the cabin, and we're not out yet, you leave." He fished in his pants pocket, extracted his truck key fob and handed it to her. "Take this."

"No way am I leaving without you and Grandpa."

"Yes, you are. If you refuse, I won't go after him."

"Aden!"

The grim determination in his face said he meant every word.

"Then I'll get him." She tried to push past him.

"No, you won't." He grabbed her by the crook of her elbow. "This isn't the time for a power struggle. You have your son to look after. He needs you."

What he hadn't said was he considered himself more expendable.

A frigid shiver seized her. "Please, Aden."

"This is my task to complete," he said. "My purpose. The reason I'm here. I'll bring your grandfather back to you, I swear."

Or die trying? She couldn't live with herself if that happened.

He leaned in close. "But I have to know you're safe

and that you'll escape if necessary. I can't cross that bridge any other way."

"What if Grandpa doesn't recognize you or refuses to leave with you? He knows me better than you and will listen to me."

"I'll carry him out."

Aden was strong, but hadn't he been coughing earlier and winded? Plus, her grandfather was a big man.

"We can go together," she insisted.

Aden shook his head. "The bridge isn't strong enough for two people. It may not be strong enough for one."

"Is that what you think?" If the bridge collapsed, there was no other means to cross.

He ignored her question. "You need to stay on this side, coaxing your grandfather to come to you. Especially if he's confused."

As much as she hated admitting it, some of what he said made sense. They would have more luck with her here. And there was the matter of the bridge's condition.

What do I do? she silently asked and remembered words from when Pastor Leonard had counseled her.

Have faith. Be strong. Don't lose hope.

Could she? Yes, she decided. She must. Life had dealt her a terrible blow. She must believe that while this trial was difficult, there would be light and joy at the end.

"All right," she said and pocketed the key fob. "But if the two of you don't appear in that doorway five minutes from now, I'm coming after you."

Aden took a step forward only to hesitate. Turning back toward her, he pressed a kiss to her lips—the contact brief but intense. "Wait for me."

Something about his expression made her think he

was talking about more than today. More than this moment.

She certainly was talking about more when she answered him. "I will."

A heartbeat later he was jogging across the bridge. He didn't look back, simply held on to the sagging handrails as he pressed ahead. Even when the bridge dipped precariously in the middle and he had to hop over a gaping hole left by a missing wooden plank, he kept moving.

"Hurry," Rayna called out, though she doubted he heard her above the fire's roar. "Stay safe. Bring Grandpa back. Bring yourself back. To me," she added softly.

When Aden reached the top of the bridge, he paused for a quick moment to regain his balance and then raised his hand to signal he'd made it. Rayna waved back and watched him sprint up the crumbling rock walkway to the cabin. He took the steps leading to the porch in two giant leaps.

At the open door, he slowed to look inside. What did he see? Whatever it was, he gave no indication. The next second, he disappeared inside.

"Let him and Grandpa—"

Rayna jerked and fell back when a tall pine tree collapsed in the woods behind the cabin. Breathing fast, she reassured herself it was too far away to cause them any harm. But what if another, closer, tree fell and landed on the cabin? The roof was no more than a collection of old, rotted timbers. It would ignite like a pile of newspaper.

"Won't happen," she said with all the conviction she could muster.

How long had Aden been gone? A minute? Two?

Rayna patted her pockets and, feeling only the key fob, groaned in frustration. She'd left her phone in the truck. How was she going to track the passing time? Should she return to the truck and retrieve her phone? No, that would be stupid.

She glanced at the fire again, felt the heat on her face and through the fabric of her clothes. Was her mind working overtime or had the flames gained on the cabin? Aden said fire typically burned uphill. But that had been proved wrong when the fire had climbed downhill to close the west road and a second time when it had encroached on the northern boundary of town. The intense and unpredictable winds were responsible.

What should she do? Rayna took a step closer to the bridge. Was that movement she saw inside the cabin? She squinted as if that might improve her vision. When hot particles blew into her eyes, she glanced away and furiously rubbed her face with her forearm.

"Aden," she shouted, but there was no reply. She tried again. "Aden!"

He couldn't possibly hear her. She patted her pockets again. Stop it! Her phone hadn't magically appeared. Her gaze traveled once more to the fire behind the cabin. It *was* getting closer! And it had begun to fan out, encompassing the ridge behind the cabin where Grandpa Will's brother met his death.

That couldn't be a sign. Unless… Were Aden and Grandpa Will in trouble? Had it been five minutes? The key fob pressed into her skin through the pocket, a constant reminder.

What should I do? I need an answer.

Colton waited at the ranch, her beautiful, precious son who'd already lost his father. Her grandmother waited, too. An old woman who might not survive the double loss of her husband and granddaughter. The cattle were there, as well. She and Aden hadn't created a firebreak around the pastures. If the fire reached the ranch, some, if not all, of the cattle would perish.

Rayna should go home. Now, before the fire advanced and cut off the roads. Aden had insisted, and he had experience in these situations.

But what if she left and then a minute later he and Grandpa Will came out of the cabin to discover she'd gone? They'd be abandoned and have no way to reach her—Aden's phone and radio were also in the truck. She'd never forgive herself if they perished.

She trembled under the momentous weight of her decision.

A mighty boom split the air loud enough it reverberated inside Rayna's chest. A tree, completely engulfed in flames and about two hundred yards away, exploded as if a stick of dynamite had been lit. The force launched burning branches high into the air. Soaring in a dozen different directions, they tumbled to the ground where they were swallowed by the fiery ground cover. Only the trunk remained standing, destroyed nearly beyond recognition. Giant blackened shards stuck out all over like sword blades where once there'd been branches, their tips burning.

The spectacle was, Rayna decided, the answer she'd been seeking. The next second she was in motion, her legs scrambling beneath her. With each step she increased her speed, heading blindly toward her destination: not Aden's truck but across the suspension bridge.

Swallowing gulps of foul-tasting air, she grabbed the

handrails, shocked at their flimsiness. Now, however, wasn't the time to chicken out.

Like Aden, she didn't look back. Neither did she glance around or above at the advancing fire. Instead, she stared down at her feet, seeing only where she needed to place her next step and not the ravine thirty feet below.

The bridge wobbled and buckled beneath her as if she was riding the back of an enormous sea creature. Lighted embers and gritty debris pelted her face and body. The pain and discomfort went unheeded. When her boot caught on a loose wooden plank, her foot went through the hole clear up to her ankle. Trapped, she fell, catching herself on the edge of a plank before she rolled off the side. She let out a scream as an arrow of pain shot up the length of her twisted leg. Before she had time to recover, a flaming branch landed beside her not six inches from her face. Screeching in alarm, she pushed it over the side to land in the bottom of the ravine.

Blood pounding, she collected her wildly scattered wits and hauled herself upright, using the nearest rope for a handhold. Turning her foot sideways, she removed it from the hole and gingerly took a step. When her leg didn't give out from under her, she continued on, clawing at the handrails, her eyes watering.

Would the bridge hold her to the end? She hadn't crossed it in…she couldn't remember when. It had held her grandfather when he arrived and then Aden. Both men were heavier than her. She should be fine. A creak sounded nearby, and she momentarily faltered. Was that the fire or the bridge? She didn't dare take the time to investigate.

Finally, she reached the last wooden plank and thrust

herself forward onto solid ground. Her muscles cried out in agony. She didn't listen and bolted up the crumbling walkway, her boots slipping and sliding.

Her focus abruptly narrowed. Everything disappeared save the open cabin door. The roar of the fire dimmed until all that remained was a low, constant hum. Over that came a strong voice urging her inside.

She quickly scaled the porch steps and rushed to the door. There, she rested a hand on the jamb and peered inside, afraid of what she might encounter. The lack of light made it impossible to see.

"Grandpa?" she called. "Aden?"

No one answered, and her panic intensified, the icy fingers once again squeezing her insides.

And then she saw them, her vison clearing to crystal sharp points.

Grandpa Will sat in the old, tattered recliner, his brother's chest on his lap and the lid open. Aden stood beside Grandpa, bent over. They were both alive!

She stepped inside, her pulse pounding.

Aden's head snapped up, and he glared at her. "Rayna. What are you doing here? I told you to leave."

Chapter Ten

Rayna rushed toward Aden and her grandfather. He should have known she wouldn't listen to him.

"What's wrong?" she demanded, her eyes wide with fright. "Why haven't you left yet?" She stopped short at the recliner where Will sat and yanked aside her scarf.

"Your grandpa refuses."

Try as he might, Aden had failed to rouse the old man. Reasoning hadn't worked. Neither had entreating. He'd just decided to wrangle Will out of the chair, throw him over one shoulder in a fireman's lift and carry him outside when Rayna appeared.

His gut had twisted at the sight of her. She shouldn't have come. Had taken a foolish risk. And yet his spirits lifted. She was here!

He snapped at her, anyway. "What in the world were you thinking, crossing that bridge?"

"You obviously need my help."

"Hi there, cupcake," Will said, interrupting them. He raised rheumy eyes to Rayna, a feeble smile on his face. "I'm just sitting here with Bernie, chattin' and waitin' on you."

"Cupcake is his pet name for Grandma." Rayna came around to the front of the recliner and faced her grandfather. "I haven't heard him call her that in ages."

"He keeps talking to that chest like it's his brother."

"Oh dear."

Oh dear? Did Rayna really not understand the seriousness of their situation? Evidently. She'd disobeyed his instructions to leave while she could.

Aden's impatience and frustration, already through the ceiling, shot higher. They had to get out of here. It was bad enough when he had only Will to worry about. How could he protect both him and Rayna?

God won't give you more than you can handle. Pastor Leonard's oft-repeated advice echoed in his head.

"I'm serious, Rayna," he growled at her. "Get out while there's still time."

"What about you and Grandpa Will?"

"Don't worry about us."

She straightened "We leave together."

"Rayna. This isn't a game."

"Aw, cupcake." Grandpa Will shuffled through the half dozen photographs in the small lockbox with his arthritic fingers. "I miss Bernie. His poor soul. He should've never enlisted."

Okay. At least he wasn't thinking Bernie was still alive and sitting in the other chair. Maybe his rationale was returning.

"Grandpa." Rayna reached down and put a hand over his, returning the photos to the chest. "We have to go. Grandma's expecting us for dinner."

He studied Rayna as if she were the one with dementia. "Grandma? My granny's been gone since the children were young'uns. You know that, cupcake."

So much for his reason returning, Aden thought. Will remained firmly rooted in the past.

"I made a mistake." Rayna hesitated and then added in a deeper voice, possibly mimicking her grandmother, "Will. It's time to leave. We can't stay."

Before she could close the lid of the chest, Will reached in and withdrew a gold cross dangling from a chain.

"We need this," he said.

When Aden would have hustled them out the door, Rayna asked, "What is it?"

Will showed her the cross. "This got Bernie home safely from the war. See the inscription? Says, 'With God all things are possible.'" He placed the cross and chain back in the chest and closed the lid. "It'll protect us from the fire. Just like it protected Bernie."

"Grandpa," Rayna said, a sob escaping.

Just when Aden thought he'd have to physically carry them both out, she took hold of his arm. Aden grabbed Will's other arm. Somehow the old man maintained his hold on the chest while they grappled with him, eventually hoisting him to his feet.

Having the chest and the cross within must have calmed him, for Will resisted only briefly before allowing Aden and Rayna to shuffle him across the cabin to the door.

"You go first," he told Rayna. "He's more likely to follow you than me."

"Should we bring wet towels or blankets?"

"No time." They'd have to locate the towels or blankets, assuming there were any in the cabin, and then draw water from the well. "They're not always effective, anyway. Especially in a fire like this one. Our best chance is to run. Fast."

"Come on, Grandpa. *Will*," she corrected herself at his startled expression and dragged him through the door.

They stopped again on the porch. The battered roof partially hid the fire raging around them. What Aden could see had him breaking out in a cold sweat. How long had he been in the cabin? Five minutes? Ten? In that short time the fire had advanced another twenty feet, surrounding the cabin on three sides. Like a scene from a disaster movie, the sky opened up to release a storm of glowing embers. Small fires sprang up everywhere the embers landed, instantly joining together to create larger fires.

Aden fought the fear growing inside him. Two people depended on him for their lives. People he cared about. There wasn't a second to spare!

He'd no sooner finished the thought than a blazing branch the size of a street sign struck the metal porch roof with a loud bang. Then another branch struck and another, the sound like bombs dropping. Before long, the old cabin would become a death trap.

"Move it," he shouted and pushed Will and Rayna ahead.

She jogged down the steps first, squawking and slapping her head when she reached the bottom, and walked straight into a cluster of embers. Will also walked into the embers, but he didn't appear to notice or care. One ignited the back of his shirt, and a small flame appeared. Aden smacked him, snuffing out the flame. Will didn't acknowledge the smack or respond.

Navigating the walkway to the suspension bridge

presented a brand-new problem. The broken rocks and uneven ground were more than Will could handle. Aden was reconsidering that fireman's lift when something inside the old man's muddled brain must have clicked for he began proceeding carefully and with purpose rather than clumsily.

"That's right, Grandpa," Rayna encouraged.

They made slow progress. Excruciatingly slow. Aden had to stop himself from yelling or shoving them along. Especially when a crash sounded from behind and Rayna wavered.

"Don't stop," he shouted above the din.

"The cabin roof just caved in," she yelled.

What concerned Aden far more than the cabin was the bridge. The same burning embers starting small fires on the ground had set the bridge ablaze. Constructed entirely of wooden planks and half-rotted ropes, it provided ideal fuel. Flames crawled along one handrail and flickered in between the planks.

In a matter of minutes, the bridge would become impassable. They only had one chance to make it across.

Reaching the foot of the bridge, Rayna turned, her face a mask of dread and uncertainty. "What do we do? The bridge is on fire."

"You go first." Being the lightest of them, she had the best chance of making it. "Run as fast as you can. Don't look back. We'll be right behind you."

"Aden—"

"Quit arguing." When she wavered, he shouted, "You have to do this. We're counting on you. Think of Colton."

That spurred her into motion, and she threw herself onto the bridge. Each time she stumbled and at each hop over a hole or flame, Aden's heart constricted. At one point, she squealed and jerked her hand away, having inadvertently grabbed a section of burning rope. He exhaled with relief when the next second she kept going.

All the while, Will stood in front of him, staring ahead. He had no idea what the old man saw, what he was thinking and if he had any inkling of the danger they were in. Hoping Will understood him, he leaned forward and spoke loudly into the old man's ear.

"Listen to me. You have to cross this bridge. Your granddaughter will be waiting on the other side. She's risking her life to bring you home to Sandy. Don't make her sacrifice be for nothing. You hear me?"

Will nodded.

"Just put one foot in front of the other." The strain of shouting and the suffocating smoke had worsened Aden's damaged throat. He swallowed against the pain. "You can do this."

Again, Will nodded. Aden wasn't sure Will had heard him, much less comprehended. But when the old man tucked his late brother's chest under his arm, Aden decided they had a slim chance of surviving.

Rayna reached the end then, and Aden nearly sank to his knees with relief and gratitude. She patted her arms and legs, extinguishing embers, but otherwise appeared to be in one piece.

"I'm okay," she shouted and waved. "Send him over."

Thank you, he whispered. To Will, he said, "Your turn," and pushed him onto the bridge.

The old man hesitated, digging in his heels. "Wait."

"There's no time."

"I never blamed you for what happened at the market.

You need to know that. You were a good kid, and you've turned into a good man. I'm proud to call you friend."

Aden's chest tightened. "Same here, sir."

With that, he gave Will another nudge. Will took one step, then another. Using his free arm, he grabbed hold of the handrail. It fell from his fingers onto the bridge and then slid over the side, the tip on fire.

"Go," Aden hollered, the emotions from a moment ago vanishing in the face of danger. "You have to take care of Rayna."

Will moved. Slowly. The bridge dipped lower and lower with each cautious step he took. Before long, it would give way.

"Grandpa," Rayna yelled from her side of the bridge and waved her arms. "Come on. Faster."

He continued at the same excruciatingly slow pace. Aden mentally hurried him along, to no avail.

When Will stepped on a flame and his pants caught fire, he stopped and bent down to pat his leg. When he straightened, he lost his balance and wobbled unsteadily, his arms windmilling. Rayna screamed. The rope handrail on the other side miraculously held when he grabbed it, and he was able to regain his balance.

Another twenty seconds lost. More of the bridge burned. The fire seared Aden's cheeks to the point of blistering. He remembered the remark he'd made to Rayna about there being no killing force more lethal than a big forest fire save a nuclear bomb.

In this moment, he believed it. Even when he was driving the bulldozer for the firefighters, the heat and destructive fury hadn't reached this level. Neither had he questioned his chances of making it out alive like he did now. He'd had dozens of firefighters and rangers in the vicinity to bail him out. What he'd give for one or two of them to show up in an emergency vehicle.

When Will reached the three-quarter point, a large burning branch fell onto the center of the bridge. He didn't look behind him, which was good, and pressed on. Rather than rolling off the side like the rope had, the branch settled into a shallow dip and remained there. Within seconds, flames leaped from the branch onto the closest rope. From there, they traveled to the nearest plank and set the dry wood aflame.

Aden's odds of safely crossing the bridge had just decreased. Will would be lucky to make it across at the rate he moved.

"Hurry, Grandpa," Rayna called.

He was near the end. Aden debated starting across and placed a foot on the first plank. The bridge shifted and rippled as if held together with string.

"Grandpa," Rayna shouted again.

Aden sensed more than saw Will cross the final few feet and Rayna haul him into her waiting arms. His focus remained riveted on the bridge and whether it would hold him.

"I've got you." Her voice carried over the wind.

The same wind knocked loose a blackened and charred plank, sending it careening down to be claimed by the ravine. Two more fell in quick succession. There were now more holes in the bridge than planks. And still it burned.

Aden knew then, short of sprouting wings, he wouldn't reach the other side. He ventured to the edge of the ravine and considered his options. The rocky side was practically perpendicular and without hand- or footholds. Even if he could climb down, there was no way he'd be able get up the other side without proper repelling equipment. Jumping wasn't possible. He'd crush every bone in his legs when he hit bottom.

"Aden," Rayna called. "Hurry."

"I can't."

Her answer was cut off when the center of the bridge gave way. It parted as if being cut by a knife, the sides smashing into the opposite walls of the ravine.

Aden crouched and shielded his face with his hands. Rayna screamed. It died on the fire's victory roar.

He scanned the area for any avenue of escape from the advancing fire. Seeing only one, he turned to Rayna, who still held on to her grandfather.

They were safe and could get home. She had the truck key.

He allowed himself a few precious seconds to commit every detail of her image to memory. It might be the last one he had of her.

The bridge had collapsed! No. Please, God, no. Don't let it be true.

And yet it was. Rayna's desperate pleas made no difference. Aden stood on the opposite side of the ravine, stranded and unable to get to her. Get home. Get to safety. Behind him, the wildfire advanced—the massive flames now devouring the cabin.

"Aden," she screamed, her voice ragged. "There's a ladder behind the cabin."

Even as she said it, she knew how insane the idea sounded. Even if he could get near the cabin, who knew if the ladder was still there? And it was a stepladder, no more than six feet tall. Useless for scaling a thirty-foot ravine.

"There might be rope back there, too."

What could he do with that, again assuming he could find the rope before the fire claimed him? There was nothing on which to anchor the rope. If by some miracle he lowered himself unharmed into the ravine, climbing the other side was impossible.

A dread like no other seized Rayna. What should he do? How could she help him? There had to be a way for him to traverse the ravine. Why was he just standing there?

Now that Grandpa Will had crossed to her side of the bridge, he'd sunk once more into dementia. As if their reality was too much to bear, he'd shrunk in on himself and clutched at her like a small child.

"Grandpa!" She flung his arm away. "Snap out of it."

He turned vacant eyes on her.

"Rayna!"

Hearing Aden's voice, she whirled. "What can I do?" she yelled over the fire's roar.

"Go home."

Go home? Had he lost his mind? "No!"

"The fire's jumped the ravine. You're in danger."

Numbly, she followed his gaze. A stand of burning trees had formed a wall of flames three stories high. Burning branches sailed across the ravine, setting the ground ablaze near where Rayna and Grandpa Will stood. Within minutes, if not seconds, they'd be trapped.

"I can't leave without you," she hollered.

Why did it seem she was forever saying that to Aden?

"You can and you will. You don't have a choice."

He'd die. She knew it with the same certainty she'd known her life was permanently changed after Steven's murder. There was no way Aden could survive this…

this…end of the world. Not without a vehicle and proper equipment.

Why hadn't she evacuated when he'd warned her and left on the cattle drive last night? Grandpa wouldn't have wandered off. She and Colton and her grandparents would, at this moment, be meeting up with the Overbecks for the final two miles to their ranch.

Aden, too, would be hard at work doing his job. He'd greet her when this was all over, sweeping her into his arms and pressing his cheek to hers.

Without warning, Rayna's entire body began to quake. She must do *something*. She couldn't lose him, too. One death was enough.

"Rayna, go!" he shouted. "You have the truck key. Get home. Save your son and grandparents. They have no chance without you."

"But you—"

"I'll be all right."

"How will you get out?"

"I have a plan."

A plan? What kind of plan? "You won't survive on your own."

"Have faith," he hollered. "I'll find a way and come back to you. I swear."

"Aden."

Her legs remained rooted in place. The fire's great roar filled her ears. Heat baked her flesh. The intense light nearly blinded her. And still she couldn't abandon him.

Dear God, help me. Help us.

Behind Aden, a flaming tree toppled and struck the cabin roof. It sent a storm of fiery projectiles into the air before the roof caved in on itself. An explosion erupted from inside the cabin. Probably the propane tank. Rayna flinched and instinctively shielded her grandfather.

Aden shouted at her again. "I can't come home and not find you waiting for me. That's the only way I can make it to safety."

The next instant, he took off, running directly into the fire, the smoke surrounding him. No jaunty wave. No tender goodbye. No flashing the grin she'd grown to love.

"Wait," Rayna screamed, but he didn't stop.

With a sinking feeling, she realized the awful truth. He'd known that as long as he stood on the other side of the ravine, she wouldn't abandon him. So he'd made the decision for her—a decision that might well cost him his life.

"Aden," she repeated his name, watching him travel farther and farther into the woods.

The woods! Not toward the fire. She blinked her watery eyes to clear them. He was heading south and *away* from the fire, though it seemed determined to catch him. He tripped over a log, briefly scrambling before resuming his run at breakneck speed.

She yelled his name one last time as he disappeared from her sight.

"Rayna, sweetheart, come on. We have to go."

The voice was calm and composed. For a second, she thought Aden was speaking to her from across the distance. Then she realized it was Grandpa Will.

"Don't let Aden's sacrifice be for nothing," he said.

"Grandpa…?" She held back the tears. He was himself again. Maybe.

"You want me to drive?" He began walking toward the walkway, leaving her at the bridge.

"No." She went after him, her frozen limbs moving at last. "I will."

Rayna took hold of her grandfather's arm and the two of them hurried as fast as they could down the walkway to where the two trucks and Claire's trailer sat parked. Sitting in the driver's seat of Aden's truck, she paused long enough to familiarize herself with the vehicle's operation and then pressed the keyless ignition button. The engine strained and then died. She pressed the button again, relieved when the engine turned over. Throwing the transmission into Reverse, she swung the steering left, executed a U-turn and stomped on the gas pedal.

Bits and pieces hammered the truck on all sides, the clatter resembling the unexpected hailstorm Rayna had gotten caught in last year. The wind, propelled by the intense heat, tried its level best to push them off the road. She was constantly required to make corrections. That, the constant howling and near-zero visibility affected her concentration. She drove by gut instinct and, she was sure, divine guidance.

How was it possible she'd left Aden behind, effectively condemning him to his death? He'd told her to go, screamed at her. Deep down, she'd realized he was right. She couldn't have helped him. Not before the fire swallowed all three of them whole.

"Steady, girl."

She glanced over at Grandpa Will, unable to discern from his expression if he'd said the words or she'd heard them in her head. For a second, she'd sworn Steven was speaking to her.

She clutched the steering wheel with shaking hands and fought to keep the truck on the road. Overcompensating to avoid a fallen tree, she drove off the side of the road. Yelping, she righted the truck and cautioned herself to pay better attention.

This was nothing, she silently chided herself as they drove. She and Grandpa Will weren't literally walking through fire like Aden.

"Please protect him," she whispered as they put another mile between them and the worst of the wildfire. "Spare him. He's a good man. Worthy of Your love. Worthy of mine."

Had she said that aloud? It didn't matter. She meant it.

Suddenly, they reached a junction with another road. Rayna hadn't seen the intersection coming and slammed on the brakes when a hulking shape materialized from the smoke. The truck skidded to a halt in the nick of time just as an emergency vehicle passed them.

She sat for a moment, her breath coming in great gusts, and her heart banging against her ribs. That had been close. Too close.

"You can do this."

Again the voice. Now, she swore it was Aden, but that was impossible. Her frazzled mind was playing tricks on her.

"Grandpa?"

He shifted in the seat to face her. "There's no turning back. You can only go forward."

People had said the same words to her when Steven died. Go forward. Move on. As if it were as simple as strolling along a neighborhood sidewalk.

But going forward was her only option. Unless...

The radio! It lay on the floor at Grandpa Will's feet. She threw the truck into Park, unbuckled her seat belt and reached past his legs. She'd seen Aden use the radio before. Many times. She could do this.

She held it to her mouth and pressed the button. "Garver District Ranger Station. Come in. This is Rayna Karstetter. Do you hear me? Come in, please." She released the button and waited. Why was no one answering?

"This is Garver District Ranger Station. Come in, Rayna. Over."

She recognized the dispatcher as the woman Aden had spoken to before. A crazy sense of relief assaulted her. "You have to help Aden. He's trapped in the fire. I'm scared he won't survive."

"Where is he?"

"At my family's cabin near Aspen Lane Crossing and…and…" What was the road number? Her mind grappled for the information. "One thirty-seven. That's it. Road 137. He was there five minutes ago. But the bridge collapsed, stranding him." Her voice grew hoarse. "He ran into the woods to escape."

"Is he on foot?"

"Yes. And alone" She bit back a sob. "He's in serious trouble!"

"Hang on a second. Out."

Had the woman lost her senses? How was Rayna supposed to just *hang on*? But she did hang on, and a moment later the woman returned.

"Come in, Rayna. Are you there? Over?"

"Yes, yes. I'm here."

"I've alerted both the local authorities and Search and Rescue."

"What are they going to do?"

"Unknown at this time."

"Nooooooo! They have to rescue him. What if he dies?"

"They'll do what they can." The woman's tone softened. "He's experienced. There isn't anyone in these parts who knows the mountains better than him."

Rayna couldn't bring herself to respond. Sorrow and despair had squeezed her throat shut.

"Are you there, Rayna?" the woman asked. "Over."

"I am," she finally managed.

"You need to go home. Right now. Are you ready to evacuate?"

"Uh-huh." She didn't want to evacuate. Not without Aden.

"Then you'd best do that. *Ahora mismo.* Over."

"Will you get word to me if they find Aden?" she asked weakly. "*When* they find him."

"*Sí.* I will. I promise. I have to go now. Over and out."

Over and out. It sounded so final.

Rayna swallowed. She had to stop thinking like that. Blinking back tears, she put the truck into Drive and looked carefully before proceeding.

She and her grandfather encountered more emergency vehicles on the road, considerably greater numbers than previously. Fire engines. Utility vehicles. Forest service trucks. An ambulance. The flurry of activity was a scary reminder of the fire inching closer and closer to town.

Had the firebreaks been constructed? Would they hold? What about the wind? Rayna peered through the smoke at the pine trees. Here, they weren't on fire. Their tops swayed, bending entirely over before snapping upright. She was no expert but judged the wind to be thirty or forty miles per hour. The worst she'd encountered in years.

What cruel trick had fate played on them? Sending record-breaking winds during a wildfire?

Twenty minutes later, they rumbled along the drive to the ranch house. The back door banged open and Grandma Sandy launched herself through it, Colton, Claire and Zip with her. Only then did Rayna remember she hadn't called her grandmother to let them know Grandpa was safe. She'd been too absorbed with thoughts of Aden and managing the road.

She pulled up alongside the ranch truck. In the near distance, the fire burned. Three miles away? Two? They needed to hurry. Except hurrying meant leaving Aden farther behind. She opened the truck door and climbed out, every bone in her body aching and her heart breaking in two.

Grandma Sandy wailed uncontrollably as she threw herself at Grandpa Will. Colton almost knocked Rayna over in his enthusiasm. Claire stood nearby, wiping her damp eyes and smiling.

"Mommy, you're home!"

Zip jumped up on her and, for once, she didn't scold the dog.

Kneeling, she drew Colton into a warm embrace as Zip licked her face. "I am. I'm home. Sorry I didn't call."

"Where's Aden?"

At her grandmother's question, Rayna stood. With each word she uttered, she felt a knife slice deep into her.

"The bridge collapsed. He didn't make it across."

"Oh, no!" Grandma Sandy pressed a hand to her chest. "Is he…did he…?"

"I don't know. He escaped into the woods. The fire was…" Rayna struggled to finish. "Close."

Grandma Sandy's eyes fluttered, and her knees buckled. Grandpa Will steadied her before she collapsed, surprisingly strong.

"He'll be okay," Colton said with a conviction none of the adults felt but wished they did.

"Yes." Rayna placed a hand on his head. "He will."

She would continue to believe that until someone told her otherwise.

"We'd best get a move on," Grandpa said. "Time waits for no man."

Rayna nodded, mustering all her willpower. She had to get her family out of here. "Colton, you help Grandma Sandy. I'll check on the animals and horses."

"You need help?" Claire asked.

Rayna recalled her last sight of the cabin. "Claire, I'm so sorry. We had to leave your truck and trailer behind."

The other woman nodded solemnly. "I figured as much."

"Yeah."

"Don't fret. I have insurance." She patted Rayna's arm. "What matters most is you and Will are home."

But not Aden. A fresh stab of agony assaulted her.

"I'll join you in a minute."

Desperately needing solitude, she escaped to the trailer, where she assured herself the goats, cats, chickens and horses were no worse for the wear. She then untied Bisbee from the side of the trailer and mounted him. Waving to Colton, who stuck his head out the truck window, and to Claire on her horse, she led the way.

Halfway to the pasture, Zip jogging alone beside her, Rayna started to cry. She was still crying when she shut the gate behind the last cow.

Chapter Eleven

Aden's ankle throbbed from where his pants had ignited. He suspected a second-degree burn but didn't bother to stop and inspect the gaping hole in the material. The fire chased him down the mountainside, always a few feet—and at times, a few inches—behind him. One glance at a rolling wave of flames bearing down on him was enough to test his courage. From then on, he kept his eyes trained ahead.

What he'd give for a flame-retardant suit or one of those portable fire shelters carried by hotshots. Anything to fend off the flames.

His knees protested each agonizing step. Bone crunched against bone. Tendons and ligaments stretched to the point of snapping. Still, gravity pulled him ever downhill. Good thing. If he were running uphill, he'd never make it. He still might not make it.

Rayna's face suddenly appeared before him. Doubtless, his last memory of her standing at the bridge, and not real. He ran toward her, anyway, his chest laboring.

Just as suddenly, her face disappeared, replaced by his destination: the creek. An eighth of a mile beyond that, Harlan's place. They'd built the firebreak around the property. No guarantee, but better than being stranded out here. He pushed harder and ran faster.

Sweat poured into his eyes, blurring his vision. For once, he was glad he'd forgotten his bandanna. With his difficulty breathing, it would have been more of a hindrance than a help. Darting between boulders and brush, he reached a clearing and discovered a narrow trail. He followed it the remaining distance to the creek where he plunged in.

Usually two or three feet deep, the previous four-month drought had reduced the flow to a mere trickle in some places. Hardly enough in which to submerge himself like Harlan had planned with the fishing hole. Instead, Aden reached down and scooped up handfuls of water, splashing them on this face and neck. The relief, though marginal, cleared his vision.

He resumed running, staying in the creek and avoiding obstacles. Whether the best decision or not, it felt safer. With every pounding footfall, water sprayed into the air. Ash filled his nostrils, the taste causing him to choke. He refused to stop and lose more precious seconds.

How far had he come? Aden couldn't be sure. Time had lost all meaning. Distance, too. He couldn't remember, was Harlan's place after the next ridge? No, farther east. Except which way *was* east? Without the sun, it was difficult to tell.

Focus, he told himself. *Keep moving*.

Yes. As long as he kept moving, he had a chance. Quitting would mean never seeing Rayna again.

Every time he was convinced he'd put some distance between himself and fire, a flaming branch would shoot past him or a tree would topple off to the side, reminding him this monster was faster and more powerful than he.

But he was smarter. And resourceful. Also determined.

Aden had something to live for and to fight for. He had someone to return home to. Rayna. She and Will had left. He'd seen them driving away in the truck, a flash of movement weaving in and out of the flames.

Why had she waited so long? He'd hated abandoning her. It was the hardest thing he'd ever done. And the most necessary. Stubborn fool. She wouldn't have left without him.

A helicopter flew overhead carrying a bucket, full or empty Aden couldn't tell. He didn't bother waving. He doubted the pilot would notice him. And even if they did, there was nothing they could do.

The next instant, a hard object whacked Aden on the back of his head. He'd no sooner registered the impact than the creek rushed up to collide with him. The world began spinning and refused to stop. Sharp points drilled into him through his clothing. He lost his cowboy hat. Unless…had that happened before at the cabin? He might have left it in the truck. Water filled his face, cutting off his air supply and rousing him. Sputtering and gasping, he lifted his head, his entire body vibrating from pain and shock.

He allowed himself a moment for the world to right itself and his racing pulse to slow, and then took stock. He'd landed diagonally in the shallow creek, his feet on one bank and his face on the other. The water felt cool after the heat of the fire.

The fire! He had to get up.

Using all his strength, he dragged himself upright to a sitting position. A twisted piece of burning branch lay several feet away, the likely culprit. If not for the creek, his hair and shirt collar might have caught fire. He didn't want to consider the outcome.

It was the incentive Aden needed to crawl to his feet, suppress the pain and start running again. The fire continued to chase him, no closer than before but no farther away.

He could do this! He *must* do this. Ten feet. Twenty yards. Fifty. Fireballs continued to rain on him like in the passages from Revelation. He swatted them aside.

Help me, Lord. I can't do this alone.

A strong push came from behind, directly between his shoulder blades. The wind? The force of the fire? The answer to his prayer?

All Aden knew was that his pace increased. Recognizing a jutting boulder, he left the creek and entered a dense thicket. A moment later, he emerged on the other side. And there it was! Harlan's place.

Aden used the last of his depleted energy to cover the remaining distance. The next thing he knew, he stood in front of the house. Instinct sent him inside where he began frantically and randomly searching. One door led to a small, pitch-black root cellar. Aden slammed it shut. He wouldn't shelter in a place with no windows and only one means of escape. The next door revealed a closet. Another hid an old washing machine.

What about the bathroom? A last resort in Aden's opinion. Pipes could burst and walls collapse.

His fatigued mind cleared, possibly because there was less smoke inside to dull his senses. What was he doing here? He had a better chance of surviving outdoors where, if necessary, he could flee. With renewed determination, he headed onto the porch—only to falter. The fire had reached the edge of the firebreak.

He scanned the immediate area. The well house was built of wood. That wouldn't do. His gaze landed on the ATV parked beneath the awning beside the house. Could he ride it through the fire? No. That would be suicide. What about the shed? The ancient car Harlan stored in there might provide sufficient protection if the flames breached the firebreak, which, at this moment, appeared likely.

What had he been told during training about hiding in a car? Close all the windows and vents, cover himself with a blanket or tarp and lie on the floor. He could do that. It just might work. The tires would explode if the fire reached him. But he'd survive exploding tires. The car was certainly safer than remaining in the open.

Aden bolted across the yard, the intense heat inescapable. Flinging open the shed door, he entered and waited for his eyes to adjust to the lack of light. Before closing the door, he took a last look at the fire, everywhere now. Fear all but paralyzed him.

Sky and earth had become indistinguishable, melding together into one giant swirl of bright orange, gray and black. Only the flames existed, determined to suck him and every living thing into their fiery centers.

He could die today. He could also survive. If the latter, he vowed to dedicate his life to good.

Find cover, the voice inside his head urged, and Aden heeded it.

Grabbing Harlan's old nylon rain poncho lying nearby, he crawled into the sedan. Positioning himself on the floor in the back seat, he covered himself with the poncho.

And then he prayed. For his safety. For Rayna's and Colton's and her grandparents'. For the residents of Happenstance, the first responders and the volunteers. He also prayed for his parents—that they be safe from the fire and, if God saw fit, find their way to Him. His brother, too.

Aden made another vow to reach out to his family again. He'd been wrong to give up trying these past years. Especially with his brother.

Lastly, he vowed to tell Rayna what lay in his heart. He hadn't believed himself capable of finding love with anyone, but he had. He loved her, and if she'd have him, he'd spend the rest of his life caring for her and Colton. The words she'd spoken to him after their kiss on her grandparents' porch returned to him, lifting and encouraging him.

A sound from outside penetrated his thoughts. The tremendous roar sounded like nothing he'd heard before. The fire. It must be close. The temperature inside the car rose higher and higher till Aden thought he would roast alive.

"The Lord is my shepherd; I shall not want."

He repeated the 23rd Psalm under his breath over and over. He lost count of how many times. Twenty? A hundred. Five minutes might have passed or an hour. He didn't know. But with each psalm he recited, he lived. The fire didn't claim him. He breathed. His heart beat. His skin didn't burn.

He paused to listen. Was it his imagination or had the roaring lessened? He levered himself up and cautiously peeled back the poncho. Yes, the roar wasn't as loud as it had been earlier. He raised his head and peered over the car seat. The shed door looked as it had. What about the rest of the property?

Aden waited another five minutes and then climbed out of the car. He cracked the shed door. When no great wave of smoke poured inside, he opened the door a few more inches.

The firebreak had held. Thank you, God! All around the property, trees and brush continued to burn but not as bad as before he'd taken shelter in the shed. The wind had taken the worst of the fire and moved on to the next section. Proceeding slowly, Aden ventured outside, jumping back when a tree toppled to the ground nearby. Too close! It breached the firebreak and sent sparks flying to land on the shed. Aden was no longer safe. He had to leave and leave immediately.

Stumbling toward the ATV beneath the awning, he glanced wildly about for the key. "Thank you," he almost shouted, spotting the glint of silver sticking out of the ignition.

Sitting on the seat, he started the engine, tensing when it cranked and cranked, died and cranked again. Finally, it turned over. He looked at the gage and released a ragged breath. Almost half a tank. He wasn't sure how many miles per gallon the old ATV got, but surely half a tank was enough. It had to be.

On impulse, he donned Harlan's purple sunglasses dangling from the handlebars. They'd reduce his visibility. They'd also provide necessary protection against losing an eye from smoldering embers. Putting the ATV in gear, he backed out from beneath the awning. He then executed a one-eighty only to sit and let the engine idle. Was driving through the fire the right thing to do? How could he be sure?

A second helicopter flew overhead, this one also carrying a bucket. As Aden watched, the bucket opened and released its load. Water fell in a long shower, dousing the flames and cutting a path through the fire.

Aden took that as a sign from above. He changed gears and gave the ATV all the gas he could. Hunkering down, he zoomed ahead, grimacing from the insufferable heat. He followed the path left by the falling water until it ended. After that, he drew on his remaining courage and plowed between a pair of burning trees.

He swore the flames licked his face, saw them grab the ATV. He hoped to God the tires didn't melt from the intense ground temperature. Then he'd be stuck and have to continue on foot. The thought made him push the ATV for all it was worth.

An error in judgment landed him in a gully. He pulled out, only to come face-to-face with a wall of fire. Making a hard right, he hit the gas, repeatedly altering his course to avoid flames and locate openings.

The ATV tried to buck him off more than once when it hit a rock or a hole. Twice, he went up on two wheels as he took a turn and nearly flipped. Standing up on the footrests and holding tight, he used his legs as shock absorbers. His sweat-soaked palms slipped off the handgrips more than once.

He decided his only chance of surviving was to go downhill, even though this fire had behaved unnaturally more than once because of the unpredictable winds. If his calculations were correct, he'd reach lumber road 164. Once on the road, he could make it to safety. And home. Where Rayna waited.

Rounding the next corner, he entered a thick patch of smoke. Driving blind, he ripped off the sunglasses and put his trust in God. When he cleared the smoke, coughing and gasping, it was to feel the ATV's tires hit the smooth surface of a dirt road. He'd made it! The trees bracketing the road were all on fire and the ever present smoke clogged the air. But the road itself remained clear. Fire couldn't burn without fuel, and dirt provided none.

He aimed the ATV southeast. Driving through a tunnel of flames, he headed toward the Dewey ranch. If Rayna wasn't there, he'd walk to Tumble Rock if necessary to find her.

Zip raced ahead, nipping at the heels of the young heifer who attempted to gore him in retaliation with her stubby horns. Zip was too fast. Rayna considered calling the dog back but didn't. Her heart was only half in the cattle drive. She operated on automatic pilot, relying heavily on her horse and Zip to pick up the slack.

Was Aden safe? Had he made it out of the fire? She'd been calling the ranger station every half hour or so to see if they'd heard any news. Each time, they gave her the same answer. Nothing yet.

Let no news be good news.

Where could he have gone on foot? She'd read an account of a man saving himself in the Yavapai Fire. He'd hidden in a deep cave that went way back into the mountainside. Were there any caves near Harlan's? Aden would know.

Swallowing a thorny knot of despair, she suppressed thoughts of him lying broken and burn—

Stop. She refused to even form the word. He was all

right. He had to be. Surely God hadn't put him in her life only to take him away so soon.

Please hold him in Your loving embrace.

Zip barked, returning Rayna to the present. The two of them brought up the rear. Grandma Sandy drove the truck ahead of the herd, the trailer's rear gate open to reveal a half dozen bales for enticement. As long as the lead cattle followed the truck and trailer, the rest would, too. In this case, herd mentality worked in their favor.

Riding along with Grandma were Grandpa Will—thankfully unharmed from his ordeal—and Colton, who, in his opinion, had never been on a bigger adventure his entire life. Rayna uttered another silent thank-you that her son was safe. The sensible part of her brain had scolded her for leaving him behind. But then, Grandpa would have surely perished in the cabin. Aden, too. She'd been forced to make a terrible, heart-wrenching decision no mother should have to.

From her vantage point atop Bisbee, she could see the entire herd stretched out ahead, the lead cattle mere specks. The maintenance road they traveled, if one could call it a road, was the width of a single vehicle and hardly more navigable than the detour Aden and Rayna had taken after being stopped at the roadblock. The cattle walked three or four abreast, mostly plodding along and sometimes engaging in small scuffles.

Claire, astride her horse, remained midpoint. Her nimble mare had no trouble following alongside the cattle, handling the dense trees and rocky ground whenever the cattle pushed her and Claire off the road.

In the mountains behind them, the fire raged. Rayna couldn't bring herself to look in the direction of the cabin, growing more and more distant with each passing minute. Above them hung an orange-and-black sky. Ash fell like snow. There was no relief from the thick smoke. Over the ridge, beyond the trees, lay the east road with its bumper-to-bumper traffic. Blaring horns carried the short distance, audible above the grunting and bellowing cattle.

Eighteen miles straight south, along the route Aden had mapped for them, waited Tumble Rock and the Overbecks' ranch. They'd arrive well past dark, having started much later than planned. All Rayna's efforts to avoid driving the cattle at night had been in vain.

She'd heard reports during the last four hours, since returning home and embarking on the cattle drive, that firefighters had built containment lines outside the north and west boundaries of Happenstance. The goal was to prevent the fire from entering the town. Billy Roy had phoned just as they were leaving on the drive and said the fire was supposedly ten percent contained. Rayna wasn't sure if that was true or wishful thinking. The ranger station hadn't confirmed or denied when she'd asked, stating there was no official report as yet.

With five miles now separating them from the fire, Rayna had started to think her crazy scheme to save the cattle was going to work. If they made it all the way to Tumble Rock, that was. They still had a long way to go and limited help. What she'd give to laugh with Aden and say, "See. I told you. Ye of little faith."

Worry mingled with fear to create a lead-like lump in the pit of her stomach. Where was he? Could he signal a plane? There were enough of them flying overhead. God willing, he'd reached the road and could flag down an emergency or service vehicle. There were plenty of those, too.

She conjured an image of Aden standing at the side of the road, a fire engine slowing down for him. He was covered in soot from head to toe but very much alive. She held that image close to her heart like a treasured keepsake.

A vehicle horn sounded behind her. With a start, Rayna spun in the saddle. Twin lights appeared in the smoke like the eyes of a dragon, dim at first and then growing brighter. The next moment, a blue pickup appeared. It was, Rayna realized, pulling a trailer. The driver laid on the horn again, and Rayna reined Bisbee to a stop.

The truck stopped, too, and the doors opened. Two men and a woman stepped out. Rayna knew them. The Overbecks! Zip abandoned the herd and trotted over for a quick howdy before returning to his duties. He didn't like the cattle getting too far ahead of him.

"Hello," Mr. Overbeck called.

Mrs. Overbeck waved. Rayna thought the lanky teenager with them might be their grandson.

"Hi." She trotted Bisbee over to greet the pleasant-looking older couple. "What are you doing here? We're supposed to meet you at the ranch."

"We came to help." Mrs. Overbeck beamed. "We tried calling but reception's terrible."

"Yes." Rayna had experienced her share of trouble getting through to the ranger station.

"Figured you could use a couple extra cowhands." Mr. Overbeck draped an arm over the shoulders of his grandson. "Brody's young and skinny as a post, but he can hold his own."

With two more people, they'd reach Tumble Rock without a problem.

"I can't thank you enough. Truly." Tears of gratitude filled Rayna's eyes.

"These are trying times," Mrs. Overbeck said. "We have to be there for each other." She glanced around. "You boys get the horses unloaded. Don't worry about dinner," she told Rayna. "I'll have a big pot of chili waiting for everyone. Whenever you get there. No matter how late."

"Sounds wonderful. Thank you again." More tears fell.

"Least we can do."

"There's a wide, relatively flat spot just ahead on the right." Rayna remembered it from the map tucked in her saddlebag. "You should be able to turn the truck and trailer around there without too much trouble."

While Rayna and Mrs. Overbeck talked, her husband and grandson unloaded their horses, already saddled and bridled. Mounting them, they joined Rayna.

"Have you any updates on the fire?" Mr. Overbeck asked.

Rayna told them about the firebreak outside of Happenstance and what Billy Roy had said about the ten percent containment.

"That's good. Heard there're some folks missing."

"Folks missing?" Rayna's voice cracked.

"Unaccounted for," Mrs. Overbeck clarified. "My guess is they evacuated and didn't tell anyone. It's not like they're lost in the fire."

Except Aden was lost in the fire. Rayna glanced away, biting her lower lip. How was she going to manage the cattle drive when her heart and mind were elsewhere? Perhaps that was why God had sent the Overbecks. She could concentrate on praying for Aden's safe return while they took care of the herd.

"Those cattle aren't waitin' for you," Mrs. Overbeck said. "You'd better skedaddle." She blew her husband and grandson kisses. "Safe travels, my loves. You, too, Rayna. See you at home." She climbed into the driver's seat.

"Where's the best place for us?" Mr. Overbeck asked Rayna.

After some discussion, they decided Brody would ride up at the front to assist Grandma Sandy and keep the herd on course. Mr. Overbeck would ride up and down the line, keeping watch for any wanderers. Rayna and Zip would continue to bring up the rear. Mrs. Overbeck followed them as far as the wide spot where, with a last wave, she turned the truck and headed home.

Once again, Rayna was alone with only Zip for company. He pranced behind the herd, constantly "zipping" from one side to the other. When a heifer or calf lagged behind, he herded them back into line, barking for good measure.

A tiny part of Rayna's brain cautioned her to prepare for the worst. The news about Aden might not be good. She didn't listen; she wasn't ready yet to accept anything other than him coming home to her like he'd promised.

Bisbee's hooves clip-clopped as he meandered along, his head bobbing. Lost in thought, Rayna didn't immediately hear the dull whine of an engine behind her. Maybe a motorcycle or, more likely in these parts, an ATV. Someone besides them was traveling the maintenance road.

She swung Bisbee around to face the approaching

vehicle, anticipation building inside her. If the person was coming fast, they might not see her and the cattle through the smoke until it was too late. She raised her arm and prepared to signal the driver—who must be near judging from the noise.

Suddenly, a dim, dark shape materialized. Fortunately, the driver appeared to be slowing. Good. They'd seen her and the cattle. Would they turn around? They couldn't pass. And if they came any closer, they might startle the cattle. A stampede could have disastrous results. They'd have a hard time regaining control of the herd once they lost it.

Rayna started to motion to the driver—a man, she could see that now—and indicate for him to go back. Something stopped her, and a hum went through her that she couldn't explain. As she squinted at the man, her heart rate accelerated.

He brought the ATV to a full stop and shut off the engine. Swinging one leg over, he climbed off, removed his sunglasses and strode toward her. The hum made a second circuit.

His face was unrecognizable beneath the grime and grunge. But Rayna would know that confident stride and those broad shoulders anywhere. She also knew that grin.

With a joyous cry, she jumped off Bisbee, letting the reins drop. She didn't care if the horse wandered off. She didn't care if the cattle went ahead without her. She didn't care about anything except reaching Aden.

Breaking into a run, she rushed toward him, shouting his name. He ran, too, pulling her into his arms and swinging her in a circle, fast and wild enough to knock her hat off. The next instant, his mouth met hers in a fierce kiss.

"You're alive," she said when they broke apart, both of them out of breath and deliriously happy. She cradled his face, desperate to confirm for herself that he was indeed real and unharmed. Not a figment of her imagination. "You made it."

"I had to find you."

Unable to stop herself, she burst into uncontrollable sobs. Aden enveloped her in the sanctuary of his embrace and pressed more kisses to the top of her head.

"It's okay, Rayna," he soothed. "Don't cry. I'm here. I'm fine."

"H-h-how did you g-g-get out?"

"I managed to reach Harlan's place. By some miracle the firebreak held, and I was able to ride out on the ATV."

She couldn't stop hugging him and buried her face in his shirt, mindless of the dirt and overpowering smell of smoke. "I prayed for your safe return."

"I prayed I'd get back to you." He pulled back and, tucking a finger beneath her chin, lifted her face to his. "I love you, Rayna. I know it's soon. Probably too soon. I don't expect you to—"

"I love you, too, Aden. I almost can't believe it, but I do."

He released a long breath, and when he spoke, his voice cracked. "I was really hoping you'd say that."

"We have a lot to talk about."

"We do. And now we have all the time in the world."

"Yes." She stood on tiptoe and gave him another sweet kiss on the lips. "Maybe not all the time. I still have to get these cattle to Tumble Rock."

"I'll go with you. I may need some of the spare gas you brought."

"You don't want to go home first?" she asked. "And what about work? The evacuation center?"

"I'm not leaving you again. Not for a long while." He gazed down at himself. "Though I wouldn't mind cleaning up a bit."

"Ride up ahead. Cut a wide circle so as not to scare the cattle. There's water in the truck, and I'm sure you can borrow one of Grandpa's shirts. Grandma will be thrilled to see you. She was almost as worried as me. Colton, too."

They weren't the only ones. Rayna hadn't noticed Zip leaving the herd until he barreled into her and Aden, knocking them off balance. Yipping and yapping, his entire body wagging, he pounced on Aden and licked his face.

"Good boy." Aden knelt down and scratched the dog between the ears.

Zip whimpered and pressed himself against Aden's chest, lavishing him with more dog kisses.

Rayna watched them, laughing. Despite what she'd once told Aden, she'd always thought the dog was a good judge of character, and he'd proved it. Even when she wasn't ready to believe it.

Eventually, Zip darted off, speeding ahead to catch up with the cattle. He was a herding dog, after all.

Aden took hold of Rayna's hand. "Come with me to the truck. I don't want to be apart from you for even an hour. I'll take the high route so as not to scare the cattle."

She could go with him, she supposed, meet up with Mr. Overbeck and ask him to replace her for a while.

Rayna would like to see the look on her family's faces when Aden rode up on the ATV.

Oh, why not be honest with herself? She didn't want to be apart from him, either. Not for an hour and maybe not ever. She'd never forget the love she'd once had, but she was at last ready to embrace a new one. Life had dealt her blows. It had also blessed her with rewards, and she'd just received another one.

She closed her eyes. *Thank you, Lord. For all that's been, for all that is and for all that will be.*

Beaming at Aden, she squeezed his fingers. "Let's go."

Together, they started walking, taking the first steps of what promised to be a long and happy journey.

Chapter Twelve

Before the fire, before Rayna, Aden wouldn't have considered attending a public gathering of this size. Of any size more than a handful of people. He'd have refused regardless of who invited him. Yet, here he was, on the lawn of Valley Community Church along with a couple hundred other people.

In those pre-Rayna days, the too-tight collar of his dress Western shirt would have been soaked with sweat and he'd have had to make a conscious effort not to fidget. Every nerve in his body would buzz—not with excitement but apprehension. The urge to escape would become too strong to resist, and he'd slip out. Preferably unnoticed.

But now, a mere two months later and with Rayna beside him, the crowd didn't bother him nearly as much. Not that Aden was comfortable or relaxed. Far from it. But neither was he avoiding eye contact or keeping to himself.

She was responsible. And the fire. Both had changed him. Healed him. Restored him. In one day, he'd walked through the valley of the shadow of death, coming out on the other side whole and unscathed and finding love with the most incredible woman he'd ever met. Aden was a lucky man, and he would never take God's gifts for granted again.

"There's the dessert table." Rayna pointed with the crook of her elbow, unable to use her hands. One was clasped firmly in Aden's. In the other hand she carried an insulated tote containing an apricot cream pie.

Who knew she was such a good cook? Aden hadn't, and he got a real kick learning new things about her every day. Turned out, she liked two-stepping, something he was passably good at. She laughed at cartoon shows almost as much as Colton, dreamed of traveling to Paris one day and went barefoot whenever possible. He couldn't wait to learn more.

"Look at all the food," she said, her eyes wide. "There are—" she counted "—ten tables."

"Yeah." Aden had trouble taking his eyes off Rayna. She wore a flouncy dress and sandals, making him think of a sunny day.

"Aden!" she scolded.

"Right. Lots of food. You hungry?"

The community had come together at the church to raise money for those who'd lost property and possessions in the fire. In addition to the potluck picnic, there was a bake sale, a canned-goods sale, a rummage sale, a craft sale, kids' games, a silent auction and raffles. Aden had purchased a pocketful of tickets at the entrance. Pastor Leonard would also be honoring the local first responders and countless volunteers who'd given generously of their time, energy and, in some cases, money.

"There's Grandma and Grandpa," Rayna said after

setting her pie on the dessert table and stowing the tote underneath with the others.

Aden followed her glance. Sandy, Will and Colton had come early and were now in the kids' area playing games. They seemed to be enjoying themselves despite Will having a rough morning.

"The Overbecks said they might show." Rayna waved to her grandparents, and she and Aden started in that direction. "I hope they do. I'd love to thank them again for their help."

During the Deweys' weeklong stay in Tumble Rock, Rayna had found a buyer for the cattle. Her grandparents' retirement fund hadn't been fully replenished, but they'd recovered enough to live comfortably for years to come. Thankfully, the ranch had gone untouched by the fire. The cabin was another story.

In a few months' time, they planned to clear the property and sell it for whatever they could get. Aden was considering approaching them with an offer if an opportunity presented itself. He liked the idea of building a house in his beloved mountains—a house he might one day share with Rayna. But he was getting ahead of himself.

The next moment, Aden and Rayna were stopped when a woman hailed them.

"Aden! *Espérame.*"

He turned and grinned. He'd know that voice anywhere. "Pilar. Hello."

The plump, middle-aged woman hurried to catch up with them. "Is this Rayna?" She put out her hand and grasped Rayna's. "*Mucho gusto.* I'm glad to finally meet the woman responsible for turning our Aden from a grizzly bear into a teddy bear."

Rayna laughed. "I'm not sure he isn't still a grizzly bear some days."

The two of them chatted amiably for several minutes as if they were old friends. Then again, they'd become acquainted during Rayna's frantic radio call to Pilar during the fire.

"Would you like to meet the Deweys?" he asked when he could get a word in edgewise. "They're over there with Rayna's son."

"Oh, yes. My husband is on his way here with our youngest. She's seventeen and thinks she's thirty." Pilar rolled her eyes. "I came straight from work."

In the kids' area, they joined Sandy, Will and Colton, who wanted to hear all about being a dispatcher from Pilar and peppered her with questions.

They shared stories about the fire, the women shedding a few tears. While a dozen homes and one ranch were destroyed, along with the McCullough homestead, Happenstance had been spared. There'd been no deaths and only a few serious injuries. All things considered, it could have been much, much worse.

The final count of lost acres totaled over two hundred thousand. It would take decades for the mountains to recover from the devastation. Nature would prevail, however, and Aden was glad to be working for the forest service. He'd be able to watch the rebirth firsthand and play an active role.

"I'm hungry," Colton announced.

"Me, too," Will agreed.

They made their way to the food tables while Pilar went in search of her husband and daughter—but not before dispensing hugs to everyone. She held on to Aden the longest.

"I'm very glad you survived." She gazed up at him with genuine fondness. "Now, go live a wonderful life and stop being such a recluse."

"I think I might." He smiled.

Pilar shot Rayna a look. "I think you might, too."

After lunch, Aden and the rest of them perused the grounds, using his tickets for the various raffles, to buy items at the craft tables, and to stock up on homemade jams. Harlan even made an appearance, relishing the attention his status as the local eccentric brought him. Claire arrived in her new truck, courtesy of her insurance company. Her new horse trailer was scheduled for delivery next week from the manufacturer.

At two o'clock on the dot, the crowd gathered in front of the church for the ceremony. Pastor Leonard stood on the steps, holding a wireless microphone. The speakers behind him carried his booming voice across the entire grounds and beyond. For a man who stood a mere five and a half feet tall, he exuded the energy and volume of someone a foot taller.

"Welcome, everyone. It cheers me to see all of you here today," he began.

Following a prayer and a brief sermon, he launched into postfire happenings and updates on the victims. He ended with how the money raised would be used.

"Now, for the part I've been looking forward to all day." He pulled a folded sheet of paper from his shirt pocket and donned his reading glasses. "There're an awful lot of folks we need to recognize and honor, as you can see." He showed the paper to the crowd. "These wonderful individuals risked their lives and put their fellow man, or woman or child, first. They didn't have to, but instead of turning their backs or looking out only for themselves, they answered a higher calling."

Applause followed each name or organization Pastor Leonard read off the list. Many were there, and they received hugs and backslaps and handshakes from those around them. Tissues and handkerchiefs were pulled from purses and pockets to dab at tears.

Aden put an arm around Rayna and rested his free hand on Colton's shoulder. Beside them, Sandy and Will exchanged affectionate squeezes. Aden closed his eyes and let contentment fill his once-empty soul. He couldn't remember the last time, if ever, he'd felt like he belonged to a family. That was something else the fire had changed.

"Now, folks," Pastor Leonard said. "There's one last person on this list I've yet to mention. Some of you here know about his feats. Those of you who don't are about to learn what someone can accomplish when God puts them to the ultimate test. Aden Whitley. Or, I should say, Ranger Aden Whitley."

Dozens of heads turned in Aden's direction. For a moment, the need to escape returned. But then Rayna smiled at him, and the need vanished.

"Aden didn't just help the Deweys get their herd to Tumble Rock and prevent them from going broke. He saved Will Dewey's life, nearly losing his own in the process."

Pastor Leonard continued, recounting the entire story of how Aden and Rayna had ventured into the very center of the fire to find Will and bring him home. He described the suspension bridge collapsing in horrifying detail, eliciting several gasps. He then told of Aden's race through the mountains mere feet ahead of the fire, him taking shelter in the car at Harlan's place—that brought a loud whoop from Harlan—and his miraculous ride through the fire on the ATV to eventually join Rayna on the cattle drive.

"It's not often we see God's work in such an incredible way. He was most certainly with Aden in those hours." Pastor Leonard searched the crowd for Aden. "I couldn't be more proud of you, son."

To Aden's surprise, a round of cheers went up for him. He dared to glance around. What greeted him weren't looks of disapproval or mistrust or curiosity. He saw only kindness, acceptance and...was it possible? Admiration.

"I'm proud of you, too," Rayna said, and her eyes reflected the love they'd expressed to each other repeatedly since the fire.

Aden was suddenly the recipient of his own share of hugs and backslapping and handshakes. Next to escaping the fire and finding Rayna, this just might be the best day of his life.

"I wish your family had come," Rayna said a little later when the event started to wind down.

"I invited Mom. She said she'd think about it, but I wasn't expecting anything."

Aden had reached out to his family after the fire. His father and brother refused his overtures. His mom, however, had responded. They'd talked on the phone a few times and met once for lunch. Small steps that might lead to more. Aden remained positive.

While he and the Deweys were strolling to the parking area, Colton skipping ahead of them, Will stopped Aden by latching on to his arm. He'd struggled at the event, drifting in and out and frequently not remembering people he'd been friends with for years. Aden had seen in their faces that the lack of recognition hit them as hard as it did Will.

"I've something to discuss with you, son. It's serious, mind you."

"Yes, sir." Aden wasn't sure if Will was in the present or the past and waited for the older man to continue.

"I want to know if you intend to make an honest woman out of my granddaughter."

Aden smiled. Will was *very much* in the present.

He captured Rayna's hand, thinking how easy it was to lose himself in her green eyes. "That's my intention. One of these days soon. If she'll have me. She's not given me any indication one way or the other."

Will snorted. "Don't wait too long."

"Oh, Will." Sandy pulled him along, sending Aden a wink. "Leave the youngsters alone to sort things out for themselves." She called to Colton, and the next second, Aden and Rayna were alone.

"Don't let Grandpa pressure you—"

Aden silenced her with a quick kiss. "He's not. I was planning on broaching the subject someday. Marriage is a big decision. It's okay if you're not ready."

She gave a soft chuckle. "I was about to say the same thing to you."

"Oh, I'm ready. In fact, I was thinking of talking with Colton. See how he feels about a stepdad."

"I'm not worried. He adores you." She kissed Aden in return. "Like I do."

He drew her into a warm embrace. "Then I guess we have some plans to make."

"I guess so." She shook her head with a mixture of amusement and confusion. "Aden Whitley. I still can't believe it. The Lord sure does work in mysterious ways."

"That He does."

Mysterious and wonderful. Aden and Rayna had both opened their hearts when they were convinced they'd never experience love or, for her, experience love again.

Happy to be leaving his past behind him forever, Aden embraced a future with Rayna. Together, the full and rich life he'd never dreamed possible stood before him for the taking. He didn't hesitate.

* * * * *

If you enjoyed this book, don't miss
Blizzard Refuge by Cathy McDavid,
coming October 2022 from
Love Inspired.

LOVE INSPIRED

Stories to uplift and inspire

Fall in love with Love Inspired—
inspirational and uplifting stories of faith
and hope. Find strength and comfort in
the bonds of friendship and community.
Revel in the warmth of possibility and the
promise of new beginnings.

Sign up for the Love Inspired newsletter
at **LoveInspired.com** to be the first
to find out about upcoming titles,
special promotions and exclusive content.

CONNECT WITH US AT:

 Facebook.com/LoveInspiredBooks

Twitter.com/LoveInspiredBks

"What about the plane?" Haley's voice squeaked like a mouse, and she clapped her mouth shut. *No one* ever saw her this scared or vulnerable.

"If we don't get out of this icy tomb, the plane won't matter." Ezra swiveled away from the safety of the wall to push her closer, then loosened the rope around his arm to lace his fingers together near her foot. "Here."

She stepped onto his interlaced hands and scrabbled up onto the frozen edge of the crevasse. Then he hauled himself up. Rain ran in cold rivulets down her face, soaking her hair, and she swiped at her cheeks as she scanned the sky.

Despite how reckless it was flying in this weather, the plane was still up there. She pointed at the dark shape now swinging around, ready to make another pass.

"They're coming back!" she screamed over the wind.

"Keep going. If we reach the rocks, we'll be harder to see."

Between her black jacket and his brightly colored gear, they were sitting ducks out on the snow. The rocks would be better than nothing.

But as they neared the edge of the ice, the plane shifted course, veering slightly east to where the sky wasn't as dark.

Taking her hand, Ezra helped her down the icy edge of the glacier onto the water-slicked, loose rock at the base of the ridge. Haley stared at the plane as it slowly circled over the area just northeast of them, ascending in altitude with each turn.

"What's that pilot doing?" Ezra yelled over the whipping wind.

"I don't kn—" She broke off, her mouth falling open, as a dark figure climbed out onto the wing and launched into the open air. Then another, and another. Five in total. Her chest tightened, her worst fears confirmed as parachutes exploded from their backs after the jumpers had cleared the plane.

Coming for *her*.

Don't miss
Hunted in the Wilderness *by Kellie VanHorn,*
available July 2022 wherever
Love Inspired Suspense books and ebooks are sold.

LoveInspired.com

IF YOU ENJOYED THIS BOOK, DON'T MISS NEW EXTENDED-LENGTH NOVELS FROM LOVE INSPIRED!

In addition to the Love Inspired books you know and love, we're excited to introduce even more uplifting stories in a longer format, with more inspiring fresh starts and page-turning thrills!

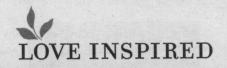

LOVE INSPIRED

Stories to uplift and inspire.

Fall in love with Love Inspired—inspirational and uplifting stories of faith and hope. Find strength and comfort in the bonds of friendship and community. Revel in the warmth of possibility, and the promise of new beginnings.

LOOK FOR THESE LOVE INSPIRED TITLES ONLINE AND IN THE BOOK DEPARTMENT OF YOUR FAVORITE RETAILER!

LITRADE0622

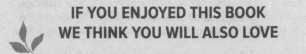